THE OHIO STATE UNIVERSITY PRIZE IN SHORT FICTION

Hibernate
S T O R I E S

Elizabeth Eslami

 THE OHIO STATE UNIVERSITY PRESS | COLUMBUS

Library of Congress Cataloging-in-Publication Data
Hibernate / Elizabeth Eslami.
    pages cm
Ohio State University Prize in Short Fiction winner
ISBN-13: 978-0-8142-7008-0 (kindle edition) ISBN-10: 0-8142-7008-5 (kindle edition)
ISBN-13: 978-0-8142-5188-1 (pbk. : alk. paper)
ISBN-10: 0-8142-5188-9 (pbk. : alk. paper)
Title. PS3605.S56H53 2014
811'.6—dc23
2013032013

Excerpt from "April" from *The Wild Marsh: Four Seasons at Home in Montana* by Rick Bass. Copyright © 2009 by Rick Bass. Reprinted by permission of Houghton Mifflin Harcourt Publishing Company. All rights reserved.

Cover design by Monique Goossens
Type set in Adobe Palatino
Printed by Yurchak Printing

∞ The paper used in this publication meets the minimum requirements of the American National Standard for Information Sciences—Permanence of Paper for Printed Library Materials. ANSI Z39.48–1992.

9 8 7 6 5 4 3 2 1

For Lyle

Perhaps we have it mixed up and it is that buried, dusty, stony earthen world below, and the time and land of sleep, that is the "real" and durable world, while the brighter noise in the world above is the dream, and the land of wraithy spirits and utmost brevity.

—Rick Bass, *The Wild Marsh*

Contents

Jocko Hollow

They are twelve and sixteen the summer two orphan grizzly cubs wander into town and pop out Peg Batchelder's windshield. It makes the papers, though not much else does.

The summer they catch their parents in the fogged up truck, run back in and pretend to be watching *Friday the 13th: Jason Lives*. That July, their dog Baby Rhino dies, and their father builds a coffin from potato boxes because he hates the thought of things eating him.

That summer they walk the ruts to the Jocko River, fed by jokes and cheeseburgers. "Growing like tall buttercup," is what their mother says, and when they climb into bed, their sleep is like a small fire burning itself out in a thicket of wet trees.

Barry carries a ziplock bag of stoneflies for Micah in his back pocket, while Micah carries the beer in an old Muralts cooler he's named Shelly. "I done packed Shelly tight," Micah likes to say, gleeful, and though Barry isn't sure why it's funny, he laughs anyway. Barry figures Micah, older by four years, is privy to certain secrets, like how their mother predicts snow with her arthritic knee.

Last night their mother forgot to fill the ice tray, so Micah padded the beer with five packs of frozen peas that crunch against each other. Barry isn't going to drink or fish, is instead going to look for arrowheads in the draw between the bald mountains. During Barry's search, Micah will drain the beers and fill Shelly with cutthroats.

It's too hot for gophers and too late in the day for warblers, only the zippering of grasshoppers through the sweetgrass, landing on their tennis shoes, wedding to the cuffs of Barry's jeans. Barry wears his brother's hand-me-downs, rolled up five times and pinned until their mother has time to hem them. A haze rises around them—the heat, their feet flattening the sweetgrass—and they break the silence by singing stupid songs.

He's an old man, in a big house, with two cars . . . and a wedding ring. Barry makes up the lyrics—sometimes it's *He's an old man, at a dead end, with a heart . . . that's full of sin*—and for some reason they pretend they're singing about their father, even though he is none of these things and has none of these things, save for the wedding ring, a dull gold band over which his skin has grown as a tree will with a barbed wire fence. They sing of their father because he's the only man they really know, except for Tim Orr who is tall and has a dead brother.

They sing of their father, of who their father might have been in another life and time. *He's an old man, with a big boat, and a fence . . . that never ends.* Barry laughs, white X's on his teeth where braces were six months before.

At the Jocko, Micah doesn't catch anything. The fish aren't there, are hiding in pools under the stone, under dead branches. Micah drinks two beers, puts his head back on the cooler, and watches Barry scrambling through the draw. Barry is exceptionally good at finding arrowheads, and sometimes finds other things besides. A flake awl, a bone scraper the year previous. A blue flint blade.

Micah opens another beer. The river is cool and fast and he can tell he's going to fall asleep. He puts his hand up to feel the hot air. The light is like another hand with its fingers between his.

The next thing Micah knows, Barry is standing over him, his head an eclipse. They're both redheads, but Barry's got the worst of it, freckles across his nose. Barry laughs with his X'd out teeth, and Micah's hand goes to his cheek, where Barry has lined up some chert shavings. Micah turns his head and they roll off into the dirt—"Boy you gone and done it," he says.

Now he has his brother by the wrist, flips him, the nothing sound of a twelve year old boy hitting the ground. Barry threatens, Barry begs, Barry squirms and barters and prays, but there's no way around it. They've performed this ritual long enough to sense when it's time, the way that Barry senses those flint blades in the draw, even while museum men from Billings explore with machines and small wiry dogs and come up short.

Micah does the singing now, holding his brother's head under. *Jocko River Lullaby, time to say one last goodbye.* Barry's eyes, big and black underwater. A cluster of fish eggs slides by his nose, his mouth pinched tight, but he does not struggle. Micah knows exactly how long to hold him before he'll start being dead. Barry's body always gets heavier, as if he's been dredged along the bottom instead of held fast in his brother's knotty little fists. Micah takes a deep breath for the both of them and yanks Barry out on the bank, where the sand sticks to him.

"Say you're sorry, Bear."

When Barry was younger and truly scared, sometimes he'd piss himself or black out, incidents that Micah would lord over him. This time he is only shaking from the cold.

"I'm sorry," Barry gasps. He reaches for the rest of his chert shavings, finds them still in his pockets.

"We should go," Micah says, collecting their mother's dripping peas. "I left you a couple of them beers. You'll have to dig through Shelly."

"I hate you," Barry says flatly, because that's what he always says, after. "I hope you die a horrible death, worse than Tim Orr's brother."

Tim Orr's brother had been on a work crew installing Les Schwab billboards on US-93 when a crossbeam dropped, slicing him shoulder to hip. He was a Gulf War vet; naturally everyone in Arlee went to the funeral. It was 102 degrees under the tent, and the minister talked about Joseph in Egypt instead of Tim Orr's brother, who was in three pieces inside a ·closed casket.

"I mean it," Barry repeats gravely. He doesn't mean it, doesn't cry anymore or tell their parents about the Jocko River Lullaby. Doesn't care really, maybe even likes it a little. Not the beginning, when his lungs burn and thud. Not the river junk in his hair or the roar of the water against his jaw. He thinks of the muskrats he and Micah sometimes find drowned under the ice.

Not supposed to be there.

The longer he's under, the less he feels. Only his brother holding him against the current, his hands like two hooks in his chest. When he emerges, he'll smell beer on Micah's breath. Barry hasn't passed out in years, but even that was nice, the world with its murky watercolor aspens whitening at the edges, a queer coiling sensation in his groin. He'd laugh underwater, thinking how their mother always said "quare" instead of "queer."

Barry and Micah walk home through the ruts. When they get there, their mother will be off to her afternoon job, their father building potato boxes in the garage. Paul Harvey carping on the table radio. Barry is pleased that he's almost dry, pleased when he realizes that they are accidentally walking in stride. He opens his hand to show Micah the shavings, pointing to each, identifying where he found it, and how. Micah's impressed. A yellow fly lands on the back of Barry's neck and Micah slaps it until it falls dead into Barry's shirt.

●

At four in the morning, they are in their mother's truck, driving through the dark vein of the pass to the Wingate Inn in Missoula, where their mother is a breakfast attendant, making biscuits and rubbery eggs from a carton. If it's slow, they sit on a stool behind the desk clerk, gnawing strips of bacon. They strip the beds, collect the trash from the housekeepers and drag the bags outside, take turns tossing them at the tabby inside the dumpster.

If there's no school, in the afternoons they follow their mother to her other job at Muralts Travel Plaza. Her boss, Will Shrimpin, lets them unclog and clean the trucker showers. Micah reaches in and brings up huge fistfuls of wet hair, throws them at Barry who yips and retaliates, spraying Scrubbing Bubbles into Micah's face.

"Don't embarrass me," pleads their mother.

Like everyone in Montana, she also holds a weekend job. A house call seamstress, but Micah and Barry rarely accompany her unless she's going as far as Missoula, in which case they wait in the truck while she goes in, the promise of Chinese takeout at The Golden Bowl. A box of thread, a needle between their mother's lips.

"Careful, Deb," warns their father. "It only takes a sneeze."

Her job is to let garments out and take them in, making allowances for pregnancies and missing limbs. She helped sew the parts of Tim Orr's brother into his uniform at the request of the funeral home, sitting alone in a cold downstairs room with stained ceiling panels.

Summers Micah and Barry spend shadowing their father, who is, during different months, a fishing guide, an animal control officer, a part-time railroad worker, and a builder of potato boxes, bird houses, and jewelry boxes he sells on the side. When school is out, Micah and Barry pack boats for men from Belle Meade and Sausalito. They help their father extricate badgers from old women's porches, rouse sleeping dogs from the middle of Dumontier Road, and, in the worst winters, shoot doomed elk who have fallen into snow graves.

Barry never leaves the truck for elk kills.

They're always alive, just their heads showing, following Micah's every move. When he approaches with his father's rifle, he can hear their legs cracking.

*

They are twelve and sixteen that summer, walking the ruts to Jocko River, Micah for his cutthroats, Barry for his arrowheads, and nothing is different except for the man with the Minnesota license plate and the dream catcher hanging from his mirror who insists on giving his beer to Micah and argues with him about wolves but then laughs and shows him a picture of his girlfriend. It looks like something torn from a magazine.

"Her name's Wren," Micah hears him say, as if from a great distance, and he watches as the guy puts his head back and lets his ponytail shake down, gold streaks like aspen leaves. Micah is having trouble focusing.

"My birth name's Hoyt. But as of today, I'm Jacques, like him that named this river. And that's . . . "—he brings his finger slowly towards Micah's chest as if to poke him, stops with his fingernail against his shirt, or maybe it just seems that close to Micah, it's so hard to concentrate— . . . "that's all you needs to *know*."

When Micah comes to, Hoyt or Jacques from Minnesota is gone. Everything is the same, the cutthroats and the peas in Shelly, a lukewarm beer by his cheek. The only difference is Barry, sitting up in the draw, blood in his pants. He is crying hard, the way Micah hasn't seen since Tim Orr's brother's funeral.

"Hey. You okay? Want me to get Dad?"

But they don't get him because Barry shakes his head. They don't do anything except try to wash the blood out of Barry's pants and underpants, Barry sitting with his thin white legs folded under him like cow bones in the sand, Micah scrubbing at the stains with his mother's peas. His hands turn purple.

Barry won't talk until they get home, and then he bursts through the door, asking for dinner.

"See any bears?" their father asks, and Barry says no, no way, José. "Let's see your loot then."

Micah disappears in the bathroom, looks at himself in the mirror and runs to the toilet. Afterward, he stares at the tendrils of blood curling in the water and listens to Barry tell their father about the blue flint knife he found, but lost.

*

They don't talk about it with each other, or with anyone. Which is fine. Everything is busy, always.

Micah takes a job washing dishes from 3–11 at The Buck Snort with a guy named Britt, the two of them scalding their arms until they look like skinned squirrels. Steek and Peg Batchelder have warned them it's only a summer job, but they know they'll get hired on again when the hunters come at Christmas. It's Arlee, and everyone knows which high school kids are reliable, who'll stick around for work after they graduate.

The Buck Snort's busy with tourists, fly fishermen and hikers who don't notice or don't care about the sign above the bar: *Environmentalists: Welcome to Montana. Please Park at Border and Walk In.*

Each time Britt gets hold of a fork, he stabs Micah. There are tine marks up and down his arm like a junkie, some threatening to bleed. Micah doesn't say anything because he deserves it, first of all, and because Britt is seventeen and crying.

"*Asshole.*" Britt wants to finish the load and take Micah outside, bust his face for taking his Josie, but here comes Josie with another stack piled high.

Josie is half Mexican and wholly in love with Micah. "*Pobrecito,*" she calls Britt, which makes him cry more. No boy, Micah knows, wants to be pitied.

Micah loves Josie back, realizes loving her means the necessary evil of taking her from Britt, who only ever managed to get her shirt open. It wasn't hard, took no machinations—she wanted to be with him. Like his mother leaving the pasture gate open to let the deer wander in.

After work, Micah is going to take Josie to his parents' place, introduce her to Barry, who's been kind of dark lately, holing up in his room with Stone Temple Pilots, but who will like Josie if he gives her a chance. Introduce her to his mother's collection of strays and to his father, making his potato boxes in the garage.

Josie leaves love marks all over his neck. Neither of them are virgins, but he feels like he's done more with her, working her warm shell with his knuckles. He's taken her to the Jocko River but has not dunked her, nor sung the weird, depressing songs about their father. Instead he brought the boom box, full of love songs. Sweet Child O' Mine. I Remember You.

Told her even about the draw between the bald mountains, pointed to the places where Barry used to find things, artifacts, but when she asked him to take her up there to look, he said no. Kissed her, said no, pulled her under him.

At the ranch that night, he holds open the gate and she walks right in. Past the porcupine eating toast in a box. Past the spitting goose and the queer deer, all bumpy and short-tempered.

"Mom's mistake," Micah says. "He was in rut, so she cut his balls." Antlers had begun sprouting out in all the wrong places. A cheek. Between the eyes. "Nature doesn't like to be fucked with," he tells her.

Twenty-eight years later, Micah and Barry will sit across from each other at The Bum Steer, the renovated Buck Snort, and pile talk on the table between them, along with three bottles of Moose Drool and two fist-sized bowls of pretzels, Micah's sunburned arm kitty-corner across the edge, his palm burning. He hasn't shared a drink with his brother in years, not since prison, not since Lee Ann was born, and his leg won't stop twitching. When he takes his arm off the table, it's so he can pull up cuticles on his thumbs, like peeling wood with a paring knife.

Barry's become spiritual since he left prison, or at least that's the word that Barry has used around Micah. He told Josie too, one night after she'd put the kids in bed and the phone rang.

"You talked to him and you didn't put me on?"

Josie said he'd called just to hear a woman's voice. "He's into that stuff my mother, she used to dabble with. Kept talking about getting his house in order, houses of the planets. *Mierda*. Crappity crap."

Now Barry is sitting across from him, searching for a memory of their parents asleep, their mother stumbling around in a robe. Their parents were always up and dressed, their mother sweeping snow off the steps or cooking, their Dad leaning against the counter with the dregs of his coffee.

"When the hell they sleep?" Barry wonders, just wanting to talk. "Always working. When you'd go to the bathroom, she'd have the bed made."

Micah downs the last of his beer, then rolls it against his forehead. "I used to climb in their bed first thing in the morning when I was sick sometimes, January, February, and the sheets was ice cold." He isn't sure what to say, what exactly Barry is looking for, or why talking about this stuff feels like walking into the basement, motor oil smells and spider webs brushing against his lips.

"There was one time with Dad, when we, when I was in second grade. You was two or three. He'd been up all night with the Orrs, shooting over coyotes to keep them off the calves. He had to talk Tim and Mike out of shooting them jokers dead. So, Dad, he doesn't get home until maybe six in the morning, comes in the kitchen and pulls out a chair. Mom, she puts a plate of bacon in front of him. No lie, he says to me, he says, "You all ready for school?" and that second he falls dead asleep, still chewing."

"No shit."

Micah considers mixing in some made-up stories, just to see if Barry can tell the difference. "That time they told us—remember, Bear—to watch *Dallas,* two episodes back to back, so they could have sex."

But Barry is staring past Micah at the television on the wall. A woman reporter talks and gestures on mute. Fires jumping through Choteau.

Barry says, "You kept on looking through the keyhole, saying, they're doing it, they're doing it! I didn't have a clue what you was talking about."

Micah laughs, his belly convulsing against the table, ketchup bottle trembling, basket of jelly. He places his palms on the sticky mat that says Soot-Away: Protect Your Family. He hasn't laughed with Barry in years, and now here is Barry across from him, a 406 tattooed on his fingers, an eye on his lower back. Here is Barry with a smoker's cough and a skinny crank body. Their parents, shadows in the keyhole, shadows by the river. The smile dies right off his face.

"Goddamn, Barry."

Barry breaks down and chews a pretzel. "Hey. Hey." He's not going to let it go dark, jabs a finger in the air to pop whatever it is building around them. "Now, I've got your blast from the past. Man, you ready?"

"Lay it on me," Micah says. He feels for some reason like crying, or at least crinkling up his face the way his boy Zeke does when he cries.

And then Barry is singing. He sings, right there at the table. *"He's an old man, at a dead end, with a heart . . . that's full of sin.* That song, and your dumbass jokes about the cooler. There's your blast. There's memory lane for ya."

Shelly, who got lost over the years. Micah looked in the bottom kitchen cabinets, down by their mother's grease pans. "Daddy, you seen Shelly?" Their father said no, no son, said he hadn't seen her, must have been you boys lost her fishing, but it wasn't.

Micah stares at Barry's finger, still in the air, the nail burned black obsidian. This man is his little brother. This man was in prison.

He takes a breath. "A fence that never ends."

"Listen here," Barry goes on. "Micah, you gotta pay some fucking attention in your life. I could have gone to the Jocko when we was boys and known that our whole lives was gonna be shit. I'm thinking, if you knew how to read it, you could look in that river and see our whole future."

Micah pulls a triangle of skin from his fingernail and drops it on the floor. *Time to say one last goodbye.*

He is sick of tiptoeing. Every conversation with Barry—even on the phone—eventually goes this way, scrabbling through weeds and gravel and dust, following shallow game trails that peter out on the rocks. Micah is going to say that Barry is shit-faced and wrong, that his life is better than Barry makes it out to be, that Barry doesn't know the first thing about him or Josie or the kids. That if Barry wants somebody to blame for his life, he better stop throwing around memories, can the drugs, get a damn job.

He leaves a ten and pushes his chair back.

It's a Tuesday in March he's supposed to pick up Barry from jail, the day before Micah's 38th birthday. "That must be a nice birthday present," the Batchelders say when they learn that Barry's about to be sprung.

"About time," is all Micah can come up with.

Josie asks Micah to go with her to her mother's before, help her flip her in bed so she doesn't get bedsores. "You know I can't do it by myself," she says, yanking a sweater over her head.

Micah lets the truck idle for thirty minutes, and sets about scraping the ice. He dug out the drive at six, but it's already icing over, little crystals in the air around his eyelashes.

No one has told him what to expect when he goes to fetch Barry. Will it be like the movies, he wonders, Barry moving through a series of larger cages toward his freedom, collecting five-year-old twenties and keys to a house that's no longer his? He has, ridiculously, an image in his head of his brother at the state prison in Deer Lodge, unmet by loved ones, speeding away on a black streetfighter.

"I ain't gonna be late for him," Micah growls as they head east.

"*Relajate.*" Josie stares out at the line of magpies on a jackleg fence, the heat blasting her cracked face. "Whatever happens, happens, like always."

After five years, Micah has adjusted to Barry being in prison. The hour and a half drive down to Deer Lodge is pretty enough, the occasional moose by the side of the road. Fall turning everything yellow in increments up the mountains. He stops sometimes for a meatball sub at Yak Yak's, makes sure he doesn't have any gum in his pockets before parking and walking to the Wallace Building.

The first time, after waiting for his questionnaire and visiting approval, he was nervous, sure of a strip search, but it was nothing, just a pass through a metal detector, a visitor badge affixed to the front pocket of his flannel shirt.

Half the time, they don't pat him down. Never even seem to carry guns.

Barry is always there already, waiting for him, uncuffed, sitting at a metal table. They are left alone in the room, allowed two hugs at meeting and parting. Once Micah brought Lee Ann, who was two, and a guard obliged when Micah asked him to take a picture of them together, Lee Ann balanced on Barry's knee.

Their parents, who have aged twenty years in five, don't ask about his visits, nor do they discuss their own. Even if Micah had the words, he wouldn't have wanted to use them. His brother some kind of drug addict, some kind of prostitute. So dumb he kept buying meth-making equipment from the same Reserve St. Walgreens.

"He was lucky," Josie said once, and Zeke turned his head, sensing that they were talking about something juicy. "He could've done a lot more time."

"Who's lucky?" Zeke asked.

"No one," Micah said.

Josie's mother's house smells slightly of urine, all the furniture and rugs covered in plastic. The midnight to morning hospice nurse has just left, the afternoon person, Scott, not yet there, and Josie scurries around, vacuuming and checking after them.

"I've got to make a run to IGA and stock her up on Boost," Josie says.

"I told you, I ain't going to be late for him."

"Jesus Mary and Joseph, we're not going to be late. Why don't you sit with her til I get back."

Micah watches her through the window, peeling out of the driveway. At the top the snow is deep, and the truck tires spin.

He doesn't want to go sit with Margarita. The death room. He doesn't like sitting with her in all that quiet, remembering his mother-in-law before the stroke. There's a sign on the front door—*No Smoking Oxygen In Use*—that makes him think all of Margarita's old timey clocks are counting down to a huge explosion.

When he does, finally, go into her room, after washing his hands in the guest bathroom, after flipping through the television on mute, she's where she always is, facing the window in the medical bed. Gray March light falls over her, over her caved-in mouth, and Micah stares at the papery sheet over her knees.

There's no reason to wait for Josie.

He slips an arm under her, grabs the sheet on the far side, and begins rolling. She doesn't smell like anything, like a concrete floor, maybe, and her white hair falls across his arm, thin and coarse as a possum's fur. What was that thing his father used to say about owls and possums and old women? He'll have to ask Barry. Barry would remember.

He is thinking just then of a night when they were boys, twelve and sixteen, following their father out into the winter night on a call. Some business to do with the railroad. "Watch Dumontier Road," their mother said. She was in her robe, drinking coffee over an old *Woman's Day*.

Micah and Barry waited in the truck cab, fighting over who would get to turn the knob to the heat, while their father ran back in for his rifle.

The truck slid a lot on the drive, its headlights cutting long beams over black ice. Micah and Barry were tired and fell quiet.

"Ain't we gonna park around back?" Micah asked, eventually.

Their father enjoyed certain railroad privileges, and Micah and Barry liked walking through the gravel lot among the other trucks and broken rails, old ties and rail grinders, the ground around them rumbling.

"Don't need to park," their father whispered. Barry had fallen asleep.

That moment Micah saw them, what was left of thirty or forty prong-horn antelope on the tracks, after the Great Northern had come through. Raw flanks, legs scattered and bent. Fluffy hind ends stained purple. From every piece, steam rose.

"They use them tracks," Micah's father whispered, even though there was no need, now they were out of the truck, closing the doors softly so as not to wake Barry, "when the snow gets too deep, you see. They use them tracks."

It had started snowing, and Micah stood there, watching his father walk through the vastation, the rifle under his arm. He lifted his legs over gut piles, heaved the biggest parts aside, shoulders and torsos, into the drifts.

Micah wanted to ask what the gun was for, even though he knew. Survivors.

·

They are twelve and sixteen, but once they were something else. The root of a tall buttercup under five inches of unbolted earth.

Barry is three and squalling, their mother running her finger inside his lip, searching for a cut or a new tooth, rotten or hiding. Their father is in the garage making owl boxes for the outside of The Buck Snort. Tourists, he says, love them owls. Owl's like an old lady, likes to watch her back. Old lady's like a possum, white hair down her crack.

Micah's mother squeezes a tube of gel on her finger and presses it into Barry's mouth, but his screams grow louder and more desperate.

"Should you of had him if you can't shut him up?" Micah asks, tearing off before his mother can come after him. She pinches his shirt on the way out, or maybe he imagines it. She wouldn't leave Barry to topple off the counter top.

Micah stops running halfway to the Jocko, once he realizes no one is after him. He walks barefoot through the ruts, old wagon trails, his parents say. His father's buzz saw skirls from behind, along with the mumble of the radio.

The Jocko is choked with spring ice, and Micah sputters into a run to its banks. He remembers being here when he was Barry's age, barn swallows scooping mosquitoes off the water in summer. Breaking up the ice with a rock, Micah sends pieces skidding across the sheet. He grabs a large shard and daggers it into the ground.

He's not sure how long he sits listening for the water slipping by under the ice. Waiting out his mother's anger, letting it dry up. When he returns, running sloppily up the hill, tears running down his face, he doesn't know what he's about to do, or why.

It is true that it's been hard to get their attention, since the baby.

Once they see he is crying, the baby long since calmed, his parents come to him, sit with him on the couch and pray, weep with him, over him, when he tells them he knows he has sinned, that his heart is too heavy for him, but a boy. For twenty minutes, they ignore Barry and tend to him, only him. The truth is what he gives them, or something not far away from it, like a cousin, a blood relative.

That he is ready to ask Jesus, or for them to ask Jesus on his behalf. That he is ready, through tears he says it, ready for forgiveness, ready for divine salvation. He tells them everything, and they believe.

Why would they not?

Muta Scale

Camilo is talking to her about his mother.

"It's big for her," he says, balancing a paper plate on his hairy knees. "Summer Slam. Night of Champions. She'll drag you by the ear to watch."

Looking at Camilo's knee is like staring at a scar, private, the skin so taut the bone shines lunar, so she looks away at Dr. Bob's children who are quietly putting fistfuls of weeds down each other's shirts. She didn't wear a bra, and it feels like warm air is under her shirt, like little fingers are poking their way under her breasts, and she's afraid of marks on her shirt and a little excited by this Camilo who's talking to her, this Camilo with two loves, his mother and wrestling.

"It's not just lucha libre, either. She watches all styles."

"That's funny," she says. "Your mother."

She has no idea what he's talking about, but she suddenly likes him better than anyone else standing around. Just to get in the car and come here, she smoked a couple of blunts, and now she regrets it. There are people and animals everywhere. Hospital picnic at Dr. Dawn's house— even the vets seem costumed, wearing layman shorts and bruises and puffy cat scratches. The air is sere with beef.

But Camilo. Camilo seems kind of blurry, or beautiful.

She has worked with him a while now but never really said anything, in this place where you can go a full day only saying things like "We'll give you a call when he's ready" and "When was the last time you noticed blood?" She's thinking she's never seen Camilo in shorts before, just the scrubs with skating penguins, a puffy jacket over them, one of those cool nights when he came in with a Little Friends application and everyone joked that he was probably an illegal. Probably got some girl to write it for him.

"Your name," she says, laughing, tugging the sticky shirt away. "I took two years of high school Spanish." She's getting breathy and stupid. "It means *The Way*."

She can't believe how stupid, how recklessly stupid she is, because now she's thinking it doesn't mean *The Way*, and she's wishing she could take him somewhere in Dr. Dawn's mansion and watch TV. That they could eat something decent out of her fridge.

"I'm not Spanish," he says, even worse. He's disgusted with her, she is sure. He stuffs a handful of Doritos in his mouth and crunches, looking at her, and she waits forever until he swallows. "You thought I was Spanish?"

She's trying to remember what Yessica said about him. That he's Filipino, that he's Mexican. That he's both. His eyes are a soft brown, as if filled in by magic marker and a cautious hand.

"My mother, she likes all styles. She'll *make* you watch."

Without realizing it, she's smiling and leaning forward so the hairs on his knees touch the bottom of her flip flops. "Haha," she keeps saying, "that's funny," even though he says everything quiet which means it sounds dead serious or like he's telling a secret. He says Royal Rumble with a straight face.

*

Three weeks he's been taking the trash out, dragging sticky bags against the backs of her legs. "You know you're supposed to use the back door," she tells him. "It doesn't look right."

Mostly he takes the trash out, though he's also supposed to clean. Take the broom to the blinds. Sometimes he'll help haul the big mutts up on the table, or lean his elbow across their necks to keep them from springing up and snapping at her when she jabs them for blood.

She smiled at him one time when he had Marie Phipps's Great Pyrenees in a headlock and she had to take its temperature and their faces were so close she could smell pimento loaf on his breath, but he didn't say a thing and she assumed he didn't like her or hated all of them for making a little more money, for how he had to clean up all their messes, all that fur like an explosion on the table.

Camilo is telling her he used to be a wrestler, only he says "wrassler." Not the fake stuff, but the stuff right out of high school, fat guys who want to graduate to the fake stuff and get rich. Camilo tells her he had a son. She didn't know that. She takes a breath and it burns inside her. "I didn't know that," she's telling him now.

"There's Paige," Dr. Bob says, walking by, touching two fingers to the back of her neck. She knows he thinks he can do this. A month ago, in his car, she put her hand down his pants, her eyes closed the whole time. He didn't blink. He never said anything, but she knew it was what he wanted. More than once he had insinuated he'd upgrade her from vet assistant to vet tech, which she knew she should be anyway since she could measure out the meds and find a vein and do anything that Vonni and Yessica could do. She knew she was more than muscle.

Whatever, she thinks. It was her decision to get in the car with him, and anyway. She had needed that money.

Dr. Bob has twin daughters who she didn't know about before today, and they're sitting in the grass, putting weeds down each other's shirts. She thinks of them on the weekends, drawing with chalk in his two car driveway.

There is a wife, too. A wife standing near Dr. Dawn, eating a hamburger with a fork.

●

Camilo has tattoos on his legs, and usually the vets make him wear long pants. He leans forward, and the plate slides a little, and she knows his hairs under it are warm even though the chicken on the plate must be cold by now. He's only eating the Doritos. There's a little bit of orange dust on his mustache.

"What happened to your son?" she's asking him. "You were talking about him like he's dead."

"Haha," Camilo says. He's looking a different way, his eyes sliding past her cheek, and then he opens his mouth and is shouting over her head to someone. "Ey! Use the can!"

The chicken slides and she pushes it back towards him with her finger, fast so he can't see.

"No," Camilo is saying to her. "He's not dead. At least not to me."

●

When they run out of things to say, she swings her feet out into the grass, away, as if she has intentions, some person to speak to or a desire for the watery vodka-y punch being ladled into plastic cups by Dr. Dawn. She's walking then, towards the giant glass windows of the house. She doesn't feel his presence dimming behind her—and she thought she might, really—only feels the coarse blades of dry grass curling over her flip flops to touch her toes. Already her feet are reddening. She's allergic to nearly everything. Milk and grass and saliva.

Dr. Bob's wife is standing next to someone's dog, trying to hug its neck, but it has stiffened against her.

She wonders if she should speak to her. If Dr. Bob's wife knows that her husband refers to his techs as "gals."

●

"Paige," someone says, shaking a plastic cup full of ice cubes. "Sit down, already."

There are fingers around her wrist, and she falls into a folding chair, metal and sagging cloth. "Hey," she says, seeing Vonni, her nose red and raw. "Have you been crying?"

"Sunburn," Vonni says, looking down at her forearms.

Vonni's in a dumb party dress, the dead skin flaking off her face and arms like shed fingernails. "You're walking around like you're lost."

"I smoked too much before coming here," she says. "It was Yessica's fault."

Vonni winces, lines forming over her nose. "Poor Yessica."

"Poor Yessica," she sighs. "Can I have some of that?"

And then she has Vonni's drink tipped toward her face, the ice cubes clinking against her teeth.

"There's nothing left," Vonni is saying. "Dr. Dawn is fixing to get everybody wasted."

Poor Yessica is their co-worker and currently Paige's roommate. Everyone says "Poor Yessica" when her name is mentioned—which is written "Jessica"—because Yessica's father died of a fast brain tumor. Yessica has been taking it hard for weeks, trying at Easter, a little halfheartedly, to climb into the tub with her father's PC.

That night Paige had sat with Yessica on the floor of the bathroom, wrapping her in one of her old green dolphin towels, the giant computer tipped over like a great head on the bathmat.

Paige isn't sure why she volunteered her one bedroom apartment. She knows when she leaves in the morning that Yessica has ample opportunity to commit suicide if she wants to. And Yessica never cries or talks about her dead father. Mostly they sit around in their Little Friends Hospital scrubs and smoke blunts and watch *The Daily Show,* smiling but not laughing, and Paige has to bite back a lot of what she could say. That Yessica's father was lucky, going fast, that Yessica herself is lucky, losing him fast, if anyone is lucky.

"Saw you over there talking to Camilo," Vonni is saying. There is no more ice in her cup. "There's a freak for the record books."

"Not really. He was eating the barbecue chicken."

"Be careful with Camilo. I guess Yessica told you. He runs drugs in those tunnels straight to Nogales. You'll be his mule."

Vonni has yellow beads of sweat above her lip like pimples.

"Not really," she says, getting up. "He was all about that chicken."

•

Dr. Dawn promises her a ride home if she can wait. She walks around the yard three times. She drinks more of the watery vodka-y punch and hugs Mrs. Phipps, who has brought her Great Pyrenees.

"I drained his anal glands," she says, a little too loud.

"You sure did," Mrs. Phipps says. "Why don't you get some bread, sweetheart?"

She excuses herself, finds one of Dr. Dawn's upstairs bathrooms and pees for a full minute, rubbing her allergic toes into the thick, pearl carpet. Tomorrow, she'll wake with hives crawling up her ankles. She'll drink a Red Bull and get Yessica to spread Calamine on cotton balls and press them to her shins.

While she's on the toilet, the door swings open and the stiff legged dog comes trotting in. One of Dr. Dawn's, the one Dr. Bob's wife tried to hug. It stares at her, discharge running black down one cheek, the pale tongue lolling over yellow teeth. The dog puts a muddy paw in her shorts, down around her ankles, and presses like a steamship against her. Shiba Inu. She's sure she's scraped it for fleas. She is suddenly peeing again in the empty echoing bathroom, the fluffy head under her chin.

•

That night with Yessica, the two of them on the floor, the computer on the bathmat running through its screensaver of galaxies, she had been thinking of her own father, whom she'd had to put in a home for people who could do most things for themselves but couldn't be trusted not to burn their houses down.

He used to call her pussy cat, and he smelled like cigars when he'd kiss her goodbye. What she remembered from being a kid was his slippers, all worn down where his toes rubbed inside them. That he was allergic too, to shellfish and bee stings. That he seemed a lot older than her mother.

When Paige was six and one of her friends asked, she told her he was twenty years older than her mother.

"He's not that much older, Paige," her mother had said, exasperated. "Good God. Not even a decade. No more than eight."

After the divorce, her mother did her best to teach her to hate him. But Paige understood her mother. She forgave her. Her mother taught herself hatred too. It made her a fighter, made her gnaw like a rat, even though she never seemed to hold the weight. Diabetic, hypertensive, hypoglycemic. Ate her way, eventually, gray faced, into supernovas in her ribby chest.

Her father was good about it, being in the home. Good natured, they said about him. He never asked how his daughter managed to pay for it. A vet assistant. Maybe he thought it was some magic stroke of government, health insurance for the only halfway poor. He was respectful.

"Somebody told me," he kept saying. "Called me right up and said your mother had a heart attack, said it right into the phone."

"She's had all kinds of episodes," she told him on the phone, eating the smoke. "She's fine. These days you can walk away from stuff."

The home smelled of band-aids, black women pushing him up to a big table for canned breakfasts, syrupy peaches and stringy pears. After dinner, someone rolled him back to his room and left him alone with the television.

When she went to see him, he was sitting on a sleeper sofa, smoking one of his cigars. Her stomach was growling and she ate a dry cookie from a plate next to his ash tray.

"They let you smoke in here?"

"Well, I can use my hands still," he said.

He asked her to sit and visit with him. And she left right then, chewing on the dry cookie, walking down the squeaky hallway, into the smell of band-aids, tread marks of wheelchairs scratched over the tiles. Hadn't been there five minutes. He had called her pussy cat when she was a kid.

If she had stayed, he would've done it again, would've kissed her on the mouth, smelling the same way all these years later. She would have cried.

All the way back to the car, her stomach was growling.

*

Royal Rumble, she's thinking. She follows the Shiba Inu out into the hallway. In one of Dr. Dawn's closets she finds a towel, and she lifts her shirt, wipes the sweat from under her breasts, and shoves the towel between stacks of folded sheets.

Inside the mansion, the air conditioning is rising from vents in the floor, moving raw silk curtains. Her skin is goose pimpled. She wraps her arms around herself and warms her fingers inside her armpits.

Down the hall, she can hear the dog's tags, the animal rolling with pleasure or itch, and when she looks inside, there is Camilo, on the bed. Of course. He claps his palms against the dog's ribcage like a kettle drum. "Hola" he's saying, again and again. "Hola, pooch."

"We scraped him for fleas, no?" He is not looking at her.

"Yes, maybe," she says, pushing her way in. "You finished your chicken?"

"I chunked it," he says. "It was getting cold."

She smiles. "I was hoping you could tell me about the Five Moves of Doom."

*

She hadn't told Yessica anything about her father in the home. Yessica never cried. Yessica's father, she imagined, died pretty because he died fast. He would have had a shaved head, cold hands. She was thinking that as they sat on the bathmat and watched the stars on the computer.

She could see Yessica's naked body under the dolphin towel, her skin looking like plastic.

Yessica was talking, her words trembling. She told her that she'd slept with Camilo. "Vonni slept with him. Outside Benchmark Cinema. Megan. And Beth at the desk."

"Jesus," she said. "Anyone else?"

"Pretty much," Yessica said.

She figured that Yessica must have been pissed to find out where she fit in the order of things, because Yessica told her she knew for a fact that

Camilo ran drugs in tunnels to Nogales, and smuggled other things. Sold Tide in bulk and cosmetics out of the trunk of his car.

"I thought he was Filipino," Paige said.

"Don't be stupid," Yessica said, pulling the towel tighter.

"I'm not," she told her. "You look like a taquito, by the way."

Paige is sitting on the bed next to him, but the dog has left. He is playing with her inflamed toes, wiggling them back and forth and rolling them between his fingers. With the air conditioning, they can't hear or smell the picnic outside, the people laughing and drinking from the pink mouth of the punch bowl. Dogs are running around, the Shiba Inu, all of them stopping occasionally, noses pointed up, smelling beef.

"I'm allergic," she tells him.

"To dogs and cats but not to me."

"Haha," she says, wishing she had a blunt. "I thought you were going to tell me about wrestling. Wrassling."

He has moved his hand up her leg, is resting it nearly on her crotch, as if he is an old mapmaker or guide, having stitched in the landmarks with needle and thread. Here is where you must go, he'd show with his fingers.

"Do you really have a son, dead or alive?"

"Haha." But his eye twitches a little, like he might be getting angry. "You already asked me that."

"Sorry."

"Um. Did you really do what they said you did with Dr. Bob?"

Her feet go numb and she goes to get up, but he squeezes her once. She is wishing she had a bra on.

And then nothing. A thermostat is ticking on. Then they relax.

"Want to go with me to Walmart?" he asks. The hand so constant she is beginning not to feel it.

Yessica had told her about Walmart. "He'll fill the basket with Tide. You'll be the distraction, so he can get out."

"Yeah. I guess. Maybe."

Yessica, she is thinking, doesn't know what she's talking about, and is probably racist. Yessica was fourth in line and will never forget it.

He has her hand and they're walking now, her bare feet in Dr. Dawn's thick carpet. Somewhere she has lost her shoes. To the grass or to one of the dogs.

Outside, the sounds are getting louder. Dr. Bob and his wife are laughing at their twins as they put weeds down each other's shirts.

She is thinking of the giant glass windows, how it seems like they're looking out, but they could just as easily be looking at her. She knows she's stupid and reckless, recklessly stupid. If she asked, Vonni would drive her home.

As they're going down the stairs, he's telling her about another wrestling thing, not a move but something. Muta scale, he calls it. A way of measuring how much blood a wrestler loses in any given match. People place bets on it, he tells her. They weigh the blood.

"My mother, especially," Camilo is saying. He still has orange dust in his mustache. "My mother," he says, his hand cold around hers. "She loves it."

Hibernators

After having enough of the world, of parties and taxes and automobiles, of parents and work and airplanes, the guy and the girl decided to hibernate. They were in love, which meant sometimes they wanted to chew each other's fingernails and eat each other's flesh, and it was hard to find time to do those things in the world, and harder still to do those things around other people, with their eyeglasses and dune buggies and business hours.

So they dug a hole.

The girl was a feminist, so she did most of the digging. Halfway through, she decided her ideas were making the ground too hard, so she fell back against the mound of loose earth, her red hair falling across the dirt like a pillowcase, while the guy took the shovel. "Now you're gonna see some dirt fly," he said, slicing into the ground. He hoped the girl would admire his demonstration of strength, proof of his health and virility. A third of the way down, the guy decided that tools were unnecessary and had led to the general laziness of mankind, so he abandoned his shovel and clawed at the ground with his hands.

"What shall we do when we get down there?" the girl wondered.

"Anything we like," he answered. What he meant was that they would be free from all expectations and that they could create their own world, underground. What he thought was that their love would bloom in the dark like the birth of a mole rat.

◆

And when they finally found their depth, the guy, exhausted, fell back upon the pile of dirt and allowed the girl to create their home. She decided to make the first chamber the baby's room. What home doesn't need a baby? She would pad it with pillows and blankets and fill it with soft, tinkling music. As she considered gender-neutral colors, she realized she had exchanged one idea for another, and she crawled up out of the hole, just enough so that her head was peeking out.

"I've fallen into a trap," she said to the guy.

"Can you get yourself out?"

"I don't know. I think it's a trap of ideas." She furrowed her eyebrows. There was dirt on her cheek, and it made the guy want to kiss her.

"If you can't get out of a trap, there's only one thing you can do," he mumbled against her lips, the dirt from her mouth crunching between his teeth. "You have to chew off your own foot."

"You're right," the girl said, disappearing back into the hole. Who needed a baby, anyway? She transformed the baby's room into a listening chamber, where she and the guy could hear predators before it was too late. She lined the walls with her uterus and ovaries and fallopian tubes, so that all sounds would be magnified.

"Excellent job," the guy said when he came in to look around.

"Thank you," the girl answered. "I'm tired. You can do the rest." She lay on her back in the listening chamber, her head snug against a pile of her own eggs, while the guy dug out the rest.

He made a sleeping chamber and an eating chamber, and a chamber to shit in. He gathered roots and the sloughed off skin of snakes for a bed, and the girl exclaimed with delight, making a sound that echoed through her hollow body and out through the hole. She ran and jumped into the bed naked. The guy followed her, bringing with him the skin of a vole he had killed with the shovel.

"This will keep us warm," the guy said.

"*I* will keep us warm," the girl answered.

The guy and the girl stayed in the bed for weeks without moving. They changed into what they wanted to become. They had thoughts, and their bodies accommodated those thoughts.

The girl wanted to contain the guy, and so she did. Without her organs, she was open and airy, and when the guy fucked her, it was like he was stirring a spoon in a tin cup. She wrapped herself around the guy and held him with her thighs, pinned him beneath her breasts, so that there was nothing to see or smell or taste but her. She opened for him, she absorbed him, and she did not miss the world.

The guy wanted to ravage the girl, to ravage her thoughts and her eyes and her body. He turned her over and over until she made sense to him, and then, when he feared he was a slave to his manhood, he cut his penis off with the tooth of a mouse and threw it up, out of the hole. When he thundered into the girl and overpowered her and held her face in his hands as if to crush it, he recoiled from himself and his ideas, and he rolled over and became submissive, letting the girl curl his hair in her fingers and trace his eyes with the blackest soil. He caused the ground to tremble with his cries of love, and he did not miss the world.

After a while, the girl and the guy left the bed long enough to eat in the eating chamber and shit in the shitting chamber. They were quick and thoughtless about these activities, often grabbing a raw worm or a maggot and shoving it in their mouths on the way back to the sleeping chamber. They were in such a hurry they did not bother to bury their feces, and eventually the hibernarium became filthy. But they did not care.

Sometimes, between fucking, they slept for weeks at a time, until their muscles atrophied and tiny spiders spun webs between their arms and legs. Ants came to live in the hollows of their bodies. Their breathing grew faint and delicate, and everything about them was still.

They did not think of the world above, unless it was because an animal was passing by, usually a deer or some other ungulate, pausing above the hole to eat grass, and then they stood still, their naked bodies pressed together, coated in dirt, in the listening chamber. Once a badger came and tried to dig them out, but the guy poked it in the nose with a sharp stick, and they were not bothered again. They took baths on occasion in an abandoned turtle shell, and when they did, they admired each other's bodies, clean and white again, if just for a moment. They fucked and they slept, and they did not dream of high-rises or of vacation destinations or of talk show hosts.

One day, the guy sat up and threw off the vole skin blanket. "I'm getting fat," he said with disgust. "I don't feel strong anymore."

"You're not fat," the girl said. "Please don't throw the blanket on the floor like that."

"Why? There's dirt in the bed already," the guy said. "Our whole lives are dirty."

"That's not the point," the girl said, shaking out the blanket.

"You're right. It's not the point. The point is I'm getting fat and weak."

The girl rolled her eyes and grit fell from her eyelashes like ash. The guy flexed his arms and looked down at his body. They both had ideas.

The guy went and built an exercise chamber. He twisted the veins of a mole rat into resistance bands, and he created a weight machine with fragments of marmot bone. He spent hours in the exercise chamber, his body accommodating his thoughts, and he did not miss the girl.

The girl, with grit falling away from her eyes, realized what a pigsty she was living in. She spent hours lining the bed with fresh snake skin and burying feces in the shitting chamber. She began to cook the meat of the insects in the eating chamber. And, while the guy looked at himself in the exercise chamber, the girl soaked herself clean and white for hours in the turtle shell, her body accommodating her thoughts. She did not miss the guy.

They both changed. It happened over time. They grew tired of sleeping.

One day the guy came in when the girl was taking a bath in the shell. She immediately covered her breasts.

"Check these out," he said, flexing his arms. "Nice, right?" The guy's arms were bigger, swollen with newly bulging veins.

"So? What's that?" she asked, motioning to his penis.

"You know what that is. Why are you covering up?"

"I was trying to take a bath in peace and quiet. Anyway, why did you put that back on?"

The guy had stitched his manhood with the thread of a mole's eyelashes.

"Because I wanted to. Because that's who I am," he said.

"I didn't know that." The girl climbed out of the shell and covered herself with part of a fox's tail.

"Now you do," the guy said.

That night, the guy pinned the girl to their bed of snake skin, and when she tried to curl his hair in her fingers and stroke him like a child, he pushed her away. He fell asleep after, but the girl stayed awake, listening in the listening chamber. She wasn't sure what she was listening for. Maybe new ideas.

For a few weeks, the guy and the girl both made trips to the top of the hole. They tried to look out, but the light hurt their eyes. They had become blind during their hibernation, and their milky eyes could not accommodate the world.

The guy tried to cook dinner for the girl to cheer her up, but she couldn't eat. "All we ever do anymore is eat grasshoppers and spider legs," she complained.

"But you need to eat. You need to fatten up," the guy said, pointing a fork with a cricket antenna toward her mouth. "Sometimes when we fuck, I think I'm going to break you in half," he said.

The girl thought about that, and then she had an idea, which at once seemed familiar to her, in a sweet way, like a lost dog. She ran into the listening chamber and took back her uterus and fallopian tubes and her eggs, and she stuffed them back inside herself.

She ran into the exercise chamber, where the guy was doing bicep curls with two naked mole rats.

"I've got it!" she exclaimed. "What if we have a baby?" She cradled her belly as if they were already pregnant.

"What are you talking about? I don't want a baby, and neither do you."

"I changed my mind," the girl said.

"But why? What good is a baby? If we have a baby, I won't be able to do my bicep curls with these mole rats, I'll always be holding the baby, and feeding the baby. I won't be able to maintain the exercise chamber at all, because the baby will wander off and strangle himself with my resistance bands."

"But the baby will bring us closer together," the girl said. "He can grow up to watch for badgers. He can listen for danger. We'll make him our forever night watchman. He'll protect us."

"We don't need him to protect us. *I'll* protect us."

"Well, maybe he'll just grow up then, and one day leave the hole. He'll go out in the world, work in high-rises and drive automobiles and wear glasses." The girl began to cry, and miniature mudslides fell down her cheeks.

The guy put down the mole rats and stared at the girl.

"I didn't know you felt this way," he said.

"Well, now you do," the girl answered.

That night, the guy and girl lay awake in bed, back to back. They didn't speak. Their heads were full of ideas, and the ideas spoke enough to make the hole tremble, and the grasses outside the hole tremble. The girl rolled over once and grabbed a handful of dirt and stuffed it down her mouth, but she gagged and spit it out. The guy clutched the baby mole rats to his chest and tried to love them, but he felt nothing, and he threw them out into the shitting chamber.

They both realized they were no longer in love, which meant they wanted to strike each other and yell at each other and will each other to disappear. And they realized too that they missed dune buggies.

There was only one thing for them to do. In the morning, they climbed to the top of the hole, the girl leading, because she was a feminist.

The guy grabbed the shovel, in case of badgers.

"What shall we do when we get up there?" the girl asked, peeking up into the light. She could barely see a thing.

The man looked up at her, his face accommodating all his sad thoughts. What he thought was, their love had died, like a collection of animals, small bones in the back of the hole. And now there was only the same world, all over again.

"Whatever we like," he said.

New Year

Over the long holiday, three of Parviz's sisters got nose jobs.

Anahita's came out perfect, like a dwarf rose floating in a porcelain finger bowl. Nasibeh, who along with her twin sister, Niloofar, had just turned twenty-one, woke to the stylish button Niloofar had wanted— a mix-up of the hospital or a twist of fate, no one would ever know. Meanwhile Niloofar's, hastily fitted with struts, would appear, once healed, upturned and overdone, as if growing toward a more distant, profligate sun.

During their week-long recovery at their grandmother's, the sisters sat wrapped in bandages and in the mystery of their new faces. Propped on silk pillows they had brought with them from Bed Bath & Beyond, they allowed Parviz and Maryam to feed them *tadig* and milkshakes while Maman Bozorg watched through gigantic glasses.

"What is wrong with my granddaughters, always rearranging themselves, bleaching their vaginas?" Maman Bozorg wanted to know. "All this for men who wear shirts open to their navels. Cock of the walk. Strutting here, strutting there."

Niloofar started laughing, then winced.

"Cut it out," Parviz said. "Unless you want to eff up your stitches." Which for some reason made Nasibeh laugh. "Maman Bozorg, see what you're doing? Don't rile them up."

"Listen to your brother," Maman Bozorg croaked, "No laughing." Even as she said it, she was yanking her grandson into a corner. "But really. Can't you do something?"

Parviz, do something? Parviz had already done the hard part, had already come all this way.

"It's what they wanted, Bozorgi." He wrestled his bicep free from his grandmother's arthritic grip and went back to playing nursemaid, forking a triangle of burnt rice between Anahita's lips.

Maryam, the youngest, fanned the twins with a *Vogue*.

"I'm nauseous," Anahita moaned.

"Thy name is vanity," Parviz told her. "And vanity must eat lest the Percocet make her puke."

*

During the surgeries, Parviz waited with Maryam, the two of them sprawled across a couple of Razi Hospital's most sadistically designed chairs. Sometimes they waited and sometimes they slept, dreaming dreams that they were still sitting, waiting. A small, outmoded television bolted into a high corner showed mostly state TV, though occasionally Parviz was roused by soccer coverage, his thumb hovering over the screen of his phone.

Maryam read Parviz's *Lord of the Rings*, jamming her bean-shaped feet into his loafers.

When her brother napped, she gently pried away the phone and dragged her fingertips over his fingerprints, blowing up maps of jungles, tree canopies magnified like bacteria. She slept some against the bloom of his stomach, and in the afternoon wandered the halls drinking from a paper cup.

Parviz never had to tell her not to go far. She was fourteen and bony, with big teeth and big ears. In seven years, she'd look like a model, like the twins, but for now she was of no interest to anyone.

Maryam cried a lot. Ever since their father, their Baba—Maryam was six then.

Good father, bad heart, their Maman had said, without any heart at all.

"Maybe she cries because she has a mother who has to make a joke out of everything," Parviz snapped.

Or maybe it was because Maman was gone too soon after Baba's death, off to the U.S., as if someone had left open the door of a cage. She only took Maryam.

"You monkeys are practically grown," she told Parviz and Anahita. "Girlfriends, boyfriends. And the twins have each other." Even though no one said anything, she continued to argue with herself on the farewell drive to Khomeini Airport. "I'll send as much money as I can. You have your Maman Bozorg, not that she's much help. Anyway, you'll see. It'll be good. Nobody wants their mother around, for sure. Mothers ruin all the fun." She laughed some strange laugh, someone else's laugh.

They didn't see their mother for eleven months. She married a professor at Pepperdine and filled his house with white furniture, their weepy Maryam, and a stocky West Highland terrier. Baba wouldn't have believed it.

After Maman fled, Parviz picked up the slack. He wasn't the best brother—he admitted that—but he paid the right people to get his sisters on the Visa lottery, then more to move them up the list. A year and a half after Baba's death, Parviz, Anahita, and the twins were in California, Parviz had met Olivia, and Maman was at least a neighbor, forty-five minutes away in good traffic.

Now, nearly a decade later, they were more Californian than not.

Still. Maryam cried, avoided school, was generally emotional—even for fourteen. When she glimpsed Niloofar and Nasibeh being wheeled away for surgery, swallowed by two massive gray swinging doors, she began sniffling. "They're taking them."

The twins, who for years had taken superficial stabs at distinguishing themselves—Nasibeh blond to the roots, while Niloofar kept her color but tweezed—had become identical once again in the confusing haze of pre-surgery, their faces dark without the usual makeup. They held hands until their stretchers were taken in opposite directions.

"They'll be fine," Parviz told Maryam. "Read your book." He had already reminded her that a million girls were probably getting something done right now, somewhere in the world. As he said it, he imagined a great, rusty dumpster behind the post-op wing, overflowing with a soup of abandoned noses and breasts.

●

Parviz's sisters had begged him to accompany them to Tehran, self-appointed capital of bargain rhinoplasty and place of their birth. It was spring break—Nasibeh and Niloofar at Irvine, Anahita a TA at Berkeley, Maryam at Uni High—and the beginning of the Persian New Year.

"We just need a driver, and maybe some light care. You're not working," Anahita loved to remind him. She had already landed a summer
internship at a design firm, building simulacra of hotel rooms with computer software, working two jobs while she carved away at her PhD.
"You've got Olivia to support you."

As if Parviz wasn't already ashamed to have been out of work for two
years, Olivia working at the lab through most of her pregnancy, everything about her snowman-like: latex gloves on her fingers, paper boo-
ties. She didn't mind working to support them, which only made Parviz
feel worse, no matter what he told himself. It was just how she was,
Olivia. When he'd first proposed, she'd leaned over him on the bed and
said: "Let's do it. Work hard, save money, go on little trips. Kids, especially. Let's be those people." It had scared him, how sincere she was, how
serious, and he'd had to stifle a laugh.

The truth was, Parviz had never held a real job. Bagging groceries,
delivering chocolate-covered fruit for a catering company. The longest
job he ever had was as a trainer at an O.C. Gold's Gym, which he had
halfway enjoyed. The deafening music, long stretches of nothing between
clients, staring across the street at an outdoor café that served blue mar-
tinis to women in tube tops. His sisters were mortified to see him with
his long hair cropped short, helping position strangers into lunges. It
was a good job, but like the others it didn't last. He let himself go, grew
a scraggly beard. Sometimes now, when the baby was asleep, he'd lower
himself to the floor to see if he could do the old abdominal crunches.

The job hadn't mattered, the way Olivia's job—her career—mattered.

After her maternity leave, Olivia's hours increased, and Parviz
scrolled through job listings, balancing Thayer on his knees while yellow
cartoon animals belched tuneless songs behind him. He quickly gained
twenty pounds.

"Job searching is my job," Parviz told Anahita. "I'm not going to jet
off for two weeks—in *this* economy—while some douche straight out of
school gets my dream job. Fuck that. So you can get an unnecessary cos-
metic procedure."

"I can show you the studies, Parviz. An attractive woman will *always*
get the job, even if she isn't as qualified as some brilliant fat person."

Parviz closed his eyes against an ocular migraine. A white egg vibrat-
ing at the edge of his vision.

"You're not really considering what I'm saying," Anahita said. She
walked across the dingy carpeting towards the fridge, dodging a col-

lection of sticky pacifiers. "This is the perfect time to take a break from all that clawing and scraping. Don't you want to see Maman Bozorg? Maman says she's not doing well. She definitely had a cyst in her knee, remember?"

"*I have a fucking infant.*"

Like a dog hearing its name, Thayer tilted his head back and looked at Parviz.

"And an excellent daycare provided by the friendly folks at Pfizer."

"Olivia doesn't like him to be in daycare. Daycare babies are at an academic disadvantage. Meaning if they grow up fat, according to you, or with lousy-looking noses, they're screwed—"

"A week and a half. Maman says she'll put you up at the Azadi. Five hundred thread count."

She bullied him into buying the tickets a week later, jiggling the baby, standing over his shoulder while he entered Olivia's credit card into Priceline.

Once you click submit, do not hit the back button. Otherwise you will be charged twice.

Two full days sitting with his sisters on planes, Los Angeles to Frankfurt to Tehran. Two days of surgeries, followed by a week of post-op at Maman Bozorg's. He had his books. He played games on his phone and scrolled through pictures of Thayer, whose first teeth were erupting. Little vampire, Olivia called him. *Waiting to see his aunts' beautiful new faces,* she texted, along with a photo. Thayer looking up expectantly, a soggy, solitary cheerio stuck to his chin.

*

Every so often Maman would text Parviz to check in on her daughters.

Poor Maryam. She needed it the most. R the others ok? Take them out for a plate of koobideh right after.

They can't eat right after.

O u said that. I need 2 come c my grandson when u get back. I bring him cucumbers.

He wants 2 eat the carpet in the upstairs bedrm. And base jump out of his crib.

O dear . . . :-(

Bottom right tooth came in. Now he has 4.

How is Saint Olivia? Maman asked.

OK. Missing conference 2 stay w/ Thayer.

What a sweetheart. U 2. U R a good brother.

Somebody had to go. Otherwise they'd come back w/ tummy tucks & brow lifts.

Maman, no stranger to Botox, made a smiley face. *Imagine trying 2 tell twins apart now. They probably asked 4 the same nose. Angelina Jolie.*

Parvis LOL'd. *Nasibeh wants 2 look like Shakira.*

New faces, Maman texted, *to face a new year.*

✦

Maryam sobbed, gulping back a ball of snot. "Anahita said that after, I would probably look like Golshifteh in *M for Mother.*"

Parviz could barely understand her.

"Anahita said—"

"Anahita's an idiot."

"How many idiots do you know who have PhDs?"

"She doesn't have it yet, Yam. And when she gets it, it won't have anything to do with noses, so you can pretty much disregard anything she says. Unless it's about architecture."

"I don't want her to know . . . " Maryam wailed. A Yahudi family cut their eyes at her.

Maryam wasn't supposed to be crying on Parviz's stomach. She was to have her nose done like her sisters.

First thing in the morning, Parviz had had to sign a consent form for her, his eyes roving over words like "clot" and "sepsis." As he signed with one hand, he grabbed Maryam's foot with the other, trying to still her trembling. Unbeknownst to Parviz, Maryam had begun the chickening out process an hour before, when the nurse affixed electrodes to her chest and stomach. By the time the anesthesiologist fed a needle into a hollow in her hand, Maryam, or scaredy-*gorbeh,* as Maman called her, was in a state and had wet the stretcher.

Dr. Hafezi clapped Parviz's shoulder. "It happens," he said. "They're really just thinking about the blood."

Somewhere, in a small room, Maryam was struggling back into her clothes.

"Should I talk to her?" Parviz wondered aloud. For all his years as an older brother, most of the time he still felt himself a bad actor, one of those lame Iranian comedians he'd see on the late night channels back home, joking about nukes. You said the things you thought you should say, tried to soften your voice a bit. Then waited to see their reactions. "Is it better if I try to convince her or something?"

Dr. Hafezi said nothing. He touched his chin probingly. "It's better if we do it when they're younger. Younger skin, younger personalities, more time to get used to it. But what do I know?"

Which seemed, to Parviz, like a strange thing for a doctor to say.

A short while later, Maryam emerged, disheveled, her bangs in a curve over one eye. "You can't tell them," she keened. "Especially Anahita."

"Don't be weird about it. They're going to be able to tell."

She hadn't needed the new nose, as if any of them *needed* a new nose. Among the girls, only Maryam had inherited Maman's elegant round-ness, her tiny pinprick nostrils. The twins with their wide noses, Parviz and Anahita with Baba's, uneven as a rutabaga. "Your nose was perfect, still is perfect." He hoped she wouldn't ask him about the ears. Perhaps she would grow into them.

"You're saying that because you're my brother."

"What about college?" Parviz asked, patting her. "Aren't you going? Maybe pre-med?" He thought of what Anahita had said about looking good for a job. Thought suddenly of Olivia, expansive in her baby weight, in her lab coat, eating a veggie wrap with the Japanese kid she was teaching, a cell splitter.

Parviz sensed he was about to say something Olivia would kill him for later. "This whole nose job business is out of control here. In the U.S., you know how it is. Smart girls only have to be smart. They don't have to look good."

At that, Maryam cried harder.

※

Although for years neither Parviz nor his mother had returned to Tehran, the sisters flew home whenever they could, staying with Maman Bozorg, making meals for her. Maman Bozorg played it up.

"My beautiful granddaughters," she said. She settled down on her worn place on the floor, the wood sighing with her.

Anahita came with the latest herbal supplements, squeezing fish oil pills between Maman Bozorg's teeth. Nasibeh and Niloofar unwrapped the gifts they had smuggled in for her, mostly old movies from the 99 cent bin they had wrapped in their panties. *Legends of the Fall. Manne-quin.* Maman Bozorg asked after her daughter and her grandson Parviz, slipping into her familiar ululation and fogging up her glasses.

What's going to happen to him? No job. Married. There are good girls here,
not like the Americans.

"Olivia is a good girl," Maryam said. "Parviz really loves her. She's a
scientist, or a lab worker or something."

Maman Bozorg sniffed. "Remind me the child's name again."

Anahita told her for the fifth time. "Thayer."

Olivia had mailed a picture of him at eight weeks. Maman prayed
over it, kissed the picture once a day. "What does that mean?"

Niloofar shrugged. "American names are different. They don't really
mean anything."

"That's not true," said Nasibeh. "There's Faith. And Grace."

"Why they didn't name him those?" Maman Bozorg asked.

At night, after Maman Bozorg had fallen asleep in her corner, the sisters
would go out to the gym to dance with other girls, to talk about boys
in America, about school and their professors. They'd reveal the new
English they'd learned. *Motherfucker.*

"Talk to that boy," Anahita said to Maryam once, because she had
never had a boyfriend. "That one, there. Samira's cousin. He likes you."

Maryam shook her head and turned away. At Uni High, they called
her "skeleton" sometimes and "ana" for anorexic.

"Go say hi."

"Shut up," Maryam said, mortified.

On their visits, the sisters saw their Persian boyfriends, their once-a-
year-boyfriends, who sent them Facebook pictures of their Persian girlfriends when the sisters were in America. Everybody worked hard to
make each other jealous. The sisters laughed and told them about their
big American boyfriends and their big American fucking, which everybody could do in public, in the streets of Tehrangeles, LA, just like
drinking and wearing sexy clothes. In Iran everybody had four or five
boyfriends or girlfriends, none of which they could do much with, unless
it was from behind, to avoid pregnancy.

On surgery week, Parviz completed the *Lord of the Rings* books and
started *The History of Middle-Earth.*

Doing his best to be a good older brother, he stationed himself in
Razi Hospital, imagining himself ennobled by his duty. He hoped he was
serving a penance. It wasn't that he hadn't tried to connect with his sisters.

But who could speak their language?

Niloofar and Nasibeh were forever chattering, whispering stories into the down of each other's cheeks. All of them—save Maryam—all of them trafficked in secrets. Night clubs, satin mini-dresses. Secret boyfriends they met up in Runyon Canyon. Parviz hated to think what he didn't know about them.

Lately though he'd been taking a more active role in his sisters' lives. He called the twins on Saturday, Anahita and Maryam on Sunday. He'd drive them to the Farmers Market and the Santa Monica Pier, buy them IKEA wardrobes for their dorm rooms. The occasional lunch out. He was trying.

"Watch they don't end up like those celebrities," Maman had said when he called to tell her about the trip.

"You're not coming?" he asked.

"I'll see that Yam is packed up," she said.

He imagined his mother standing in the center of the professor's house, the modern white furniture spaced out over an expanse of hardwood floors. Her shiny life. He could imagine the look on her face, her mind turning over. How happy she was to have proven Maman Bozorg wrong.

"You're going to leave me in charge of them? You want me to unleash those girls in the Gandi District?"

"Please. They'll be busy with pre-op and post-op when they're not actually under the knife. It'll probably be a relief to have all of them unconscious. You know I've got to help Edward with the syllabus," she told him.

"I'm not the one they want with them. They need their mother."

"Anyway," she said, settling the issue. "I can't bear to see them all cut up like that."

*

One by one, the sisters woke from their chemically induced slumbers, bruised princesses glittering under tubes and the spells of modern medicine. They were told not to laugh or smile or use straws, to make rest and healing their first priorities. They would have little time to heal before getting back on a plane to return to school.

"You do realize everyone else will have tans and bikini lines, and you're going to have tape all over your face?" Parviz had asked on the Frankfurt-Tehran flight.

"Oh my God, Parviz, you really don't know anything," Niloofar said. "My Media Studies prof has Restylane injections every month. You should hear her try to say 'acoustic environment.'"

Parviz drove his sisters back from the hospital, only leaving them unattended while he went to fetch painkillers and extra gauze; even then, they were never aware they were alone. When he came back to the car, he found Anahita asleep with her head against the seat, breathing through her mouth. Only Nasibeh stayed awake from the beginning of the procedure through the trip to Maman Bozorg's, later claiming she had felt the doctor gently hammer back the pieces of her cartilage, like repairing a delicate historical ruin.

He didn't stay long at Maman Bozorg's, long enough to see them through the first couple of days of recovery. He didn't know what he was afraid of exactly, but he was glad his sisters were too doped up to ask.

"I'll pick you up Thursday morning. Be ready or we'll miss our flight." He handed them a bag with their medications. "Maman Bozorg will make sure you take these. The directions are on the bottle. And the doctor says don't touch your bandages. Maman knows some surgeon back home who'll check that everything looks okay." He glanced at Maryam and Maman Bozorg. "You'll call if they start acting up?"

His grandmother nodded.

"Don't be such a hen," Anahita said, barely moving her lips.

"Mind if I come over later?" Maryam asked. "I'll take the bus."

"Fine," said Parviz. "I'll be at the Azadi, 204. Call if anybody needs me."

As he pulled out into traffic, he saw Maman Bozorg's head hanging out the window staring down at him.

＊

Parviz had been there when Maman and Maman Bozorg had their big blowout. Three weeks had passed since they'd buried Baba. It was blazing hot, the windows open, and they were fighting in whispers so as not to inform the whole neighborhood.

"I love you, I sacrifice myself for you, but I'll tell you something," Maman vented. "You are wrong about everything."

Maman Bozorg wept, fogging up her giant glasses. "Probably you are right. But promise me when you get there and find yourself surrounded by bad people doing bad things, you will think of your poor mother here, all alone with her teapot."

Maman collected her bags and smoothed her clothes. She had spent good money on new luggage and a Brazilian hair straightening treatment and felt unstoppable. "I promise."

"And then you'll come back."

Maman peered out the window at the neighbors walking on the roof, letting their three forbidden dogs pee off the side of the building down on someone's sheets. She didn't miss her husband, her *eshgheman,* and knew she wouldn't miss this.

"*Khoda hafez,*" Maman said. When she said goodbye, she meant it.

Maman Bozorg didn't bother to walk her to the door. She stayed in the corner, talking to herself. "And then you'll come back," Maman Bozorg prayed, to no one, to the walls, her mouth in a perpetual pucker. Maman Bozorg had married at thirteen, raised eight children in a dirt floor house she shared with her husband's family in Zarabad. She had long ago come to the edge of her knowledge.

Maman tried to smile. "You don't get all the way to America just to turn back around."

"Then you will be miserable," said Maman Bozorg.

Parviz showered off the hospital smell and collapsed on his hotel bed. Somewhere across the city, his sisters were sleeping on a pile of blankets on Maman Bozorg's floor, a sticky web of narcotic dreams beclouding them. When the drugs wore off, they'd be sore and swollen, maybe a little confused. They'd look pretty ugly before they looked pretty.

There were to be psychological complications in the weeks ahead, after the bandages came off. They would catch themselves in the mirror, said Dr. Hafezi, in the windows of stores.

Parviz thought of his grandmother's face hanging out the window, the bruise of her mouth. He could still see her as he pressed himself into a mountain of pillows. He had entrusted his sisters to a ninety-year-old woman whose only knowledge of medicine involved prayer and rosewater.

Before he knew it, he had slept an hour or two, more than he had since arriving in Tehran.

In the evening, Olivia popped up in a window on his laptop, wanting to Skype. It was eight in the morning in Irvine, and she thought they could feed Thayer his breakfast together.

The light from the bay window cast a diagonal bar across her neck as she leaned forward.

"Well, how was it?" she asked. "Are they happy and beautiful?"

"It was *Saw*. Plastic Surgery Edition. Gruesome."

Olivia laughed and turned away, spooning oatmeal on Thayer's tongue. *Loll, loll, loll,* Thayer said after each swallow.

When she got as much as she could into him, Parviz knew she'd lift him up by his armpits and wipe down the highchair, the hem of her thin blue robe sweeping through uncollected trails of crumbs.

For some reason he recalled a pair of pink platform sandals she wore on their first date, the edges scalloped like an oyster holding the pearl of her foot. Her pale skin and pale eyes, a transparency to her. She'll never lie to me, he thought.

"They're like welterweights, but they'll look better when they heal."

"Poor things."

"Dow!" Thayer shouted, banging his fists against the plastic table.

Parviz smiled at Olivia, just a flicker, like an accident. He wanted to ask her if she found it as depressing as he did to be home all day, the baby DVDs with their shrill music, strong-arming the wheels of Thayer's stroller down the apartment steps. How tired you could feel, doing nothing. He didn't ask, of course. Because he knew. She was grateful for the time away from work, grateful to be with their child. She was, he thought, so incomprehensibly patient.

"Mowy!" Thayer shouted again, waving his arms frantically. "Dow!"

"Hold on," Olivia said. "I'm going to send you a picture of him. He wore his big boy pants yesterday."

"The ones your mother got him?" Big boy pants. Parviz reached down and squeezed his fat roll.

But Olivia was up, after her phone in another room, having never heard him, or never answered. She left the baby in front of the computer, where he continued to hammer his fists for a few seconds, his face threatening to dissolve into a mask of frustration. Abandonment. In another moment, however, he was fine, and even seemed to notice Parviz on the screen.

"Hey Thayer, hey buddy," Parviz waved, but the baby quickly looked away in the direction Olivia had disappeared.

There was a knock on the hotel room door, and Parviz got up to let Maryam in. She was already rolling her eyes.

"Everything okay over there?"

Maryam sat on the bed next to him. "Nasibeh's out cold, and Niloofar and Maman Bozorg are watching *Point Break*. Hi Thayer!" she called, waving to the baby.

"What about Anahita?"

"Anahita's on the warpath because she forgot the Internet connection here is so fuzzy."

"She should be resting, for fuck's sake. Hey, Thayer's teeth are coming in, did I tell you? Olivia calls him 'little vampire.'"

"I can't believe he already has teeth," Maryam said, yawning, curling up with her back to Parviz. "I thought they get those at three or something."

"Apparently not. This is a picture of him in his new pants. Gift from his granny."

"Maman?"

"Yeah, right. Olivia's mother."

Ellen, who arrived early for babysitting, smelling of hand lotion. He'd left Thayer with her more times than he cared to admit, accepted money from her, even when it wasn't necessary.

T. misses you, Olivia texted suddenly. *Are you still flying back Thursday?*

She hadn't, he realized, said *she* missed him. He could barely see her, her waist behind Thayer's highchair, the phone in her hand.

On schedule 4 Thursday, he texted.

He flipped through the photos Olivia kept sending, one after another. Thayer in a collared shirt and khakis, a part in his hair. Thayer on a wagon. A studio shot at the "North Pole," wearing a turtleneck, surrounded by cotton batting for snow.

"Do you think it's weird I didn't get a nose job?" Maryam asked.

She was so quiet, he'd thought she had drifted off. He turned around to look at her.

"I think it was smart. You didn't need one anyway."

"But they're all going to look beautiful," she said, yawning again. "And I'll look different."

"You look beautiful," Parviz said, catching her yawn. He exhaled, touching his stomach. "You know you look like Maman. You're the only one. The rest of us look like Baba, Baba's big fat nose."

He thought of his father at the beach in Kish. Baba's hair in a black ponytail down between his shoulder blades like a snake. Wearing his tight white pants. Parviz was six, Anahita one, and Baba was teaching him to swim. Parviz was terrified, the saltwater splashing into his mouth.

"Hold on to my shoulders," Baba said, ducking into the green water so Parviz could climb on his back. "Baby birds ride between their mother's wings. You get here, between my wings."

Maryam shivered. "What if I stayed here? With Maman Bozorg."

"Bozorgi can barely take care of herself. Plus, you have school. Look, Yam, see his teeth? Four of the suckers."

"Parviz?"

His phone buzzed again: *This is his new jumper. I took him to see Amanda and her kid Caden across the street. He loved it.*

"Parviz."

"What?"

He texted back: *That Caden seems slow for his age, no?*

"What if I said I was pregnant."

Maryam pushed herself harder into him, until he could feel her spine along the length of his.

Maybe a month before Thayer was born, Olivia came home in a good mood. She was huge by then, needed help sitting and standing sometimes, but she still had a meager buzz of energy, like a low watt bulb.

They sat together at the kitchen table in front of her laptop.

"I emailed this to myself," she said.

It was a high resolution scan of a 10 week old embryo's face. A ridged, shapeless mass, two dark holes for eyes. A metamorphosis, sped up, like footage of a blade of grass sprouting from the ground. For a second, it looked like a pumpkin. A crack became a mouth. Suddenly there were nostrils dropping from the crown of the head, eyes moving flounder-like from the side of the head to the middle. The lip rose from the jaw. It widened. It built and rebuilt, each second becoming more recognizable.

Unfolding, revising, erasing all mistakes.

Victory Forge

I.

The boy sends home three letters from Basic, where they are making him into something. His words are pieces, insect legs in sandy loam.

He takes to the military quickly, memorizing the Soldier's Creed, believing the religion that all things can be improved. He eats their good food and wakes to their song. Wasn't it only yesterday that he sat in a wooden chair on the first day of kindergarten, his fingertips inside the dry spine of a picture book? He's over six foot now, the same child in a different uniform. Says he should've been born into his ACU trousers instead of skin.

Patriot, gunfighter, warrior. He works a strange tongue, though he hasn't yet left for Afghanistan. Fire rate. Recoil. Electronically enhanced M16. He has buddies now from Texas and South Dakota, places he's never been to or thought about. Battle buddies, he calls his friends, the second word to soften the first.

Each morning he slips an abridged bible into the pocket over his heart. When he was a kid he believed in Kurt Cobain and vampires. Late nights in the trailer, he would kneel on a brown carpet and say his prayers to a dusty ceiling fan.

It's been four months now, three letters and a photograph on Facebook. Shorn down to stubble, he is fresh born. Faded slightly in his uniform, like a daguerreotype. The hair is gone from his face. No more music, no huffing. No weed.

For the first time ever, he's standing up straight.

II.

You can't trust what you don't understand, and what you don't understand are those skinny boys hanging around the sliding glass doors of Walmart and the tech schools, sitting with their hands hidden under folding tables. If you don't mind, they'd like to ask you a couple of questions about your future.

They came in the spring, when the first flowering pears were bursting like snow clouds. They asked you about your plans, and when you said your plans were to burn a flag while flipping David Petraeus the bird, they asked you about your boyfriend's plans.

"He's my little brother, shithead. What makes you think I have a boyfriend?"

The one with the purple face laughed.

You were going to tell them to fuck off, but the boy answered them. He took shiny brochures and cards with their names. They shook his hand and offered a solid imitation of respect. A lopsided smile crept up the boy's face.

III.

That summer at the movies, the Army commercials played before the previews. Troops standing in formation. Between tight shots of soldiers' faces, soft and blank as cotton, there were men and women in camouflage fatigues boarding a helicopter. Repelling down an icy cliff. Hoisting the American flag.

"What bullshit," you whispered in his ear.

"You don't understand. It's about sacrifice. It's about something greater than yourself."

"What's greater than yourself?" You choked down a fistful of popcorn and stared at the greasy jut of his chin. "What else do you have if not yourself?"

"Country." He said it like it was a girl's name, some girl he had a crush on, someone he followed home after the street lights popped on along Bucktown Lane.

What about college? You couldn't even ask. He was never going to college, any more than you were.

The voiceover meant business. Army Strong.

He's right. You don't understand. You don't see the sense in giving your children away, getting a flag in return. A dinner napkin with sharp corners. Some consolation prize.

IV.

There are rules for receiving letters in Basic, like in prison.

He does twenty-five push-ups before they'll hand him the first one, warm Southern earth blooming between his fingers. When you forget to use a flag stamp, they yell into his cheek while he does a fifteen minute hold. The human table.

From his bunk, he memorizes the staccato drilling of a woodpecker in a longleaf pine. He takes a mental inventory of the contents of his sack: sleeping bag, tent, helmet, canteen, shovel, bullet resistants.

The boy doesn't tell you this, but he has convinced himself he is a machine. He feels the euphoria of being dismantled and reconstructed, of becoming part of a platoon. He loves these people more than he's ever loved anyone, including you, including Mama and Daddy. Love that burns up all memory. You are only his sister, a peripheral nothing. Of you he thinks: Go back to Olive Garden and the Startown Cineplex, where you make sense.

You stare at a maroon stain on one of his letters. Is it food or blood? When you sent him a beer cake it took you four hours to make, they made him run six miles after watching his squad leader eat it. Not even a bite.

The platoon is pretty cool, the food pretty good, nothing is too bad so far. He adds "so far" to the end of almost every sentence, like a constant flinch. He jokes about getting killed but says he's having a good time and he hopes you are too. You think he must be high. You pretend he's at extreme summer camp.

He doesn't know who won *American Idol* or *So You Think You Can Dance?* Those are the kinds of things you write about in your letters. Alyssa Milano's pregnant. The new Batman movie has that beautiful French girl with the gap between her teeth. It looks awesome, even without Heath Ledger.

His world in the bottom of the country is divided into heat categories and quarts of water consumed, his overlords drill sergeants who seem tall and empty at the same time. They take pains to learn how to say his name, allowing him one chance to correct them. His name is all he gets to keep.

V.

Three months before Basic, he slept with a girl. He wouldn't talk about it, but you knew she was his first. First girlfriend, first everything.

Summer Belue. Porn star name, but a good girl from decent parents. Her mother worked at a Wells Fargo, chubby fingers sliding twenties through a metal drawer. The girl's father did something at one of the plants, another man inside the roar of machines. There were two or three Belue brothers you would see now and then, pumping gas or buying cigarettes Friday nights at the Walmart Super Center, trying to start up conversations with people in line.

The first time you saw Summer, you and the boy were eating at Ryan's Buffet. She came in with her parents, stood behind them holding a warm plate against her chest, her hands clouded by the steam of mashed potatoes. A reedy blond ponytail, jean shorts with heart pockets, flip-flops smacking against the dirty bottoms of her feet.

A vein pulsed in the boy's neck.

"That your girl?"

"Shut the fuck up." He shoved a dinner roll in his mouth.

Summer sat with her parents near the door, but she kept coming up for more corn on the cob. She looked at the boy through the foggy glass of the buffet, smeared with two hundred spaghetti plate dinners. The boy's acne scars lit an angry red.

You're pretty sure he had sex with Summer Belue. You don't know when, or if he used anything. Sometimes they'd just go in his room and hold hands with the door open, listening to old Nirvana bootlegs, playing video games. "No ma'am," Summer would say if you offered her iced tea or Pizza Bites. You're only six years older, but still: No ma'am.

One night, maybe two weeks before he delivered himself to the military, he came out of the room, his hair stuck to his neck like streaks of oil. Summer emerged shortly thereafter, a fresh coat of makeup painted over her chin. You clicked off the remote and stared at them. Outside on the gravel lot, the day laborers' kids were setting off fireworks three weeks late.

They both looked at the floor as Summer walked to the kitchen to dump a half finished can of Sprite down the sink. "See you at Mozer's," she said to him. After she left, he went back in his room and shut the door.

You thought for a while maybe Summer Belue was enough to change his mind. Maybe he'd stay behind, stay inside her on her parents' sticky water bed, trading kisses. Maybe he'd fuck up and get her pregnant, help raise the bay-by.

She couldn't hold him. Nor his friends, his drug dealer in the vintage Mustang, the endless cans of Four Loko and dub sacks you left on his bed.

You were grateful when Summer Belue came to the mall to say good-bye. Even if she didn't say anything to you, no "no ma'am," no nothing, just sat there holding his hand under the table, smacking her flip flops against the soles of her feet. She stared at a group of shrieking girls in front of the Game Stop.

The recruiter handed him a clipboard. "Pretty girlfriend."

"She's not my girlfriend," the boy said.

VI.

In a month, he's in the weeds.

Virtual rifle simulation. Combatives. Pugil sticks. Dummy grenades.

Time shares in a computerized Iraq City, where he learns to clean houses. Be a sharp shooter. Collect badges like a Boy Scout.

He warns you not to respond to his letters because he'll no longer receive them. He tells you, don't worry, he has war heroes watching over him, guiding his hand when he removes the idiot proof plug on his rifle. Patton, Schwarzkopf, McChrystal.

While you ferry bread baskets and lunch plates to old women at Olive Garden, he ferries ammo across a broken bridge. Both of you fake your way through it. Faking runs in the family. Mama pretending she could raise children. Daddy bluffing his way into bed with a bottle blonde surveyor, even before he divorced Mama. Nothing is real, no ma'am.

The boy wants to graduate to live fire, to three days in the woods of Victory Forge. Laser tag and buddy team movements. Men streaking through the bones of dead trees, their hearts baptized in a stream sullied with sediment, blessed by the flicking tongues of unseen animals.

He is proud when he tells you of his worst twenty seconds. Twenty seconds in a real CS gas chamber, gagging, nose dripping, eyes burning.

He managed to cough out his name, social, and rank better than most. He endured. He thinks if he can survive that, Victory Forge will be a piece of cake.

You take that letter from your pocket and feed it down the garbage disposal at work. You push it deep, down past sodden noodles and cold grains of rice. When Javier asks if you have another batch of dishes for him, you don't answer. Your fingers are bleeding.

VII.

Is he hiding? What is his fear?

VIII.

Summer Belue's got another boyfriend, but you don't write that in the letters. Some guy who looks exactly like her brothers, works as a smoke-jumper. Walks around town with his knuckles digging between her shoulders, like he's feeling for a lost key at the bottom of a lake.

IX.

It was one year ago Daddy came over with his girlfriend while Mama was at work. You all watched *The Hurt Locker*. Daddy and the boy ate peanut butter cups on the couch with the cat between them, swishing her fat, gray tail. That cat used to attack the boy in his sleep, claw his face bloody, until Daddy kicked her across the room.

When the movie was over, they sat at the kitchen table, Daddy telling stories of Vietnam. Growing up, he would always get quiet when you asked if he ever killed anyone. Just give you a look, like you ought to know better than to ask. He sat there talking about the soldiers in *The Hurt Locker*, his face like an old sea captain. There was chocolate all over his chin, but no one said anything.

You felt bad for the bottle blonde surveyor standing around by herself in the kitchen, locked out of the conversation, so you went over next to her but there was nothing to say. You could never remember her name. Mama called her "that bitch with the tripod," and for the life of you, that's the only thing you could think of. This woman standing on street corners, orange metal legs splayed out in front of her.

"I want to work EOD," the boy said. "I think that's my calling."

You smacked him on the back of the head. "That was a movie."

"No one asked you. I'm gonna be EOD, diffuse bombs. Fuck yeah, I am."

"That James was a cowboy," Daddy whined, "that ain't like it is in real life," but there was no convincing him.

His eyes had turned. You knew that he'd stopped thinking. That he was becoming. Eater, killer, death bringer.

Daddy got quiet, disappeared into the bathroom for a long time, kept flushing the toilet and washing his hands. The Tripod brought him some gin and closed herself in with him, and they commenced whispering for five or six minutes. They left soon after when Tripod convinced him to go for a drive, Daddy looking as ashamed as he had when he kicked the cat.

When everyone was gone, you locked the door and closed the blinds.

"I swear to fucking God, I will kill you before you set one foot in the military."

The boy sat there quietly eating the rest of Daddy's peanut butter cups, kicking the legs of the table where you used to wipe your boogers.

"I'm not joking. I will beat the shit out of you before I let you blow yourself into pieces because of some goddamned Hollywood movie adrenaline-junkie death wish."

He wouldn't answer. He squeezed the candy wrappers in his fists.

You washed dishes, listened to him kick the table. The neighbors were just coming home, their headlights crawling across the yard, past the monkey grass, over Mama's wormy cabbage heads.

"You care if I eat this last one?" he asked, his mouth full.

X.

In his letters, he writes that he is fine so far. He is going to the ranges all the time in preparation for Victory Forge. He is proud, having just run two miles in 15:15. He is taking a step forward, but he doesn't say where he's going or how long it will take him to get there.

His first letter was signed "Love, Brian." The last he signed with only his name.

Sour Milk

He was born with a blond pompadour in Comanche, Wyoming to raconteurs and pitiable circumstances. His father had just finished serving out the last months of a jail stint for writing bad checks and masterminding an elaborate pyramid scheme; his mother was a secretary for a shady utility company and spent her free time downing boxes of pink wine. They brought Deacon Friddle home from the hospital and installed him in the trailer like an imitation wood coffee table.

The infant lay drowsily in his crib, while his parents both snapped open purple cans of Tab. Jack and Jenna Friddle were unsurprised and uninspired by their baby, as they had been by the pregnancy, which they mistook for months as gut fat.

"How soon do you think we can tell if he's 'special'?" his mother wondered.

"Let's hope he's not," Jack Friddle said, leaning over the baby.

The rest of their parenting could adequately be described as hands-off.

They rented a trailer on a month-by-month basis from a woman with a brown dog chained outside. She usually rented to migrant workers who roomed five to a trailer and split the two hundred dollar rent, or disappeared before it was due. The woman, Mary-Beth Unruh, had white-blond hair and deep vertical lines down her cheeks. She also had few expectations in life, so used was she to being swindled.

Like the Friddles, like most everyone in Comanche, Mary-Beth viewed life as a vast, flat plateau. Everything that you saw was everything that you ever would see, past and present, unless you went and did something stupid to put yourself over the edge. She didn't bat an eyelash when the Friddles brought home their baby to a trailer that smelled of migrant sweat and barbed wire, with flesh-colored asbestos leaking from the closets, though she did feel quite sorry for the child.

Deacon grew up terrified of Mary-Beth Unruh. She was always coming over to yell at his parents, mostly his mother—his father would be gone soon, off to drive semis in the desert with an Indian named Kathy—for not paying their rent. His earliest memories were of his mother placing him belly-down on the green shag carpet, trying to buy another free week in the trailer. He couldn't crawl yet, but he'd lace his fingers through the carpet and bawl. He remembered his mother's toes out of their work heels, all gnarled up, and the dirty tennis shoes of Mary-Beth Unruh. Words were exchanged, voices raised, all bouncing from the fake wood walls.

Mary-Beth Unruh knew that Jenna Friddle brought out the baby for sympathy, let him drag himself around on the floor, but it worked anyway. Sometimes she got the rent, and sometimes she didn't. Either way, when she was leaving, she'd pick Deacon up and jiggle him a bit. "Po, po, pitiful thing," she'd say. "How'd you get so pitiful?"

*

Deacon was afraid of the dog chained to Mrs. Unruh's trailer. When he was older, his mother would send him with a roll of twenties to pay toward the rent, and he made sure to give the dog a wide berth. It was a mix of something, yellow with a small head and big body, seemingly always pregnant, with big, purple nipples that hung down to the ground. The dog's name was Martha the Terrible.

One time, a few years after his father left for good with the Indian, Deacon went over with fifty bucks. He was twelve. Outside was a stocky, dark-haired man smoking vigorously on the steps of the Unruh trailer, with what looked like fur on the tops of his hands. Deacon had never seen him before. He wore a shirt that said Comanche City Volunteer Fire Department. In smaller print, it read Beware: Oversized Hose. The man flicked ashes off into the gravel, and Martha the Terrible gobbled them up, her tongue stained black.

Deacon wasn't paying attention and made the mistake of surprising the dog. Its head swung around like a hammer. Martha really only nipped him, her teeth pinching the back of his hand, but he screamed for five full minutes, even after the man kicked the dog in the ribs and it ran back yipping to its ashes. "Cut it out," the man said, shaking Deacon by his skinny shoulders. "It ain't like she took your whizzer."

This is how Deacon met Mary-Beth Unruh's husband, Grandad. Grandad Unruh was not a grandfather, it was just that everybody called him that. His real name was Kim.

Deacon figured it was a safe bet no one would have mistaken Grandad for a grandfather anyway. He was a womanizer who dyed his beard brown to match his hair and liked telling dirty jokes and playing the lottery with his wife's money. He was a fraud, like Deacon's parents. None of them were what their names suggested them to be. False advertising. It shook off them like gold dust.

Grandad Unruh had a separate place a little ways down into the divide, a small thorny ranch.

Mrs. Unruh used to live down there with him until he started getting on her nerves, not to mention the cheating and the lotto. She had been a teacher at the tech college in Cheyenne, and she used her savings to buy the first trailer for herself as a vacation home away from Grandad, and the other trailers as an investment. Then she bought Martha the Terrible as a guard dog after the migrant workers tried to rob her, and after Grandad tried to get back in her bed. Fortunately for Mrs. Unruh, the dog hated migrant workers; unfortunately, it liked Grandad, who brought it elk legs he found up in the mountains, with muscle and fur still attached.

Deacon grew up with the Unruhs. They understood his parents were losers without ever acknowledging it in any way. They paid him a little something to help out at the ranch. His mother didn't care, so he went, sometimes for hours after school. Grandad showed him how to prop up the sheep for vaccinations and shearing. Deacon loved the heavy feeling of their wooly backs pressed against his legs, like suitcases.

*

Deacon was a smart boy. Eventually, he noticed the ranch beginning to fail, and Mrs. Unruh beginning to fail.

The dog died first, after crawling under the back wheel of the trailer. You could smell it before you got close to the trailer park. Mrs. Unruh called Grandad in tears, and he came over to get it, pulling it slowly out by the chain. Deacon stared down at Martha, who didn't look like Martha anymore. She didn't even look much like a dog. Small flies made determined inroads beneath the skin around her eyes.

"Goddamn, they don't wait long, do they?" Grandad said. "Wanna help me bury her?" He wrapped his furry fingers around the handle of the rusty shovel he had used to kill the marmots Martha only maimed. Even Martha was a fraud that way, not finishing the job, leaving the sandy things flopping around, all bloody and legless.

Grandad showed Deacon how deep to make the hole. To discourage the wolves.

"Might as well bury Mary-Beth at the same time, she's gonna be so broken-hearted," Grandad said. He was right.

After the death of Martha the Terrible, Mrs. Unruh never came over to ask for the Friddles' late rent, or for anything.

*

In a few years, Deacon grew up. His mother liked to say it was all the milk and clean Wyoming air, but that was a lie, like all things. The air around the trailer smelled of oil, rust, and waste from the nearby ranches, and most of the time, the milk was sour, unless it was the chocolate milk Deacon bought with money he took out of his mother's purse, the chocolate tending to stay good longer. Deacon got to over six feet tall pretty quickly, and his blond pompadour scraped the low trailer ceiling. He developed something like muscles, small lumps at intervals down his pale arms. Everyone in high school looked at him like he was an alien.

"Does anybody smell horse shit?" the boys would laugh when he walked into class.

Deacon never talked to anyone. He got to school late and left early, hurrying back to the Unruh's, though lately that place was equally depressing.

Mrs. Unruh was well on her way toward senility. Her eyes were cloudy, like she could see into the future. Sometimes she held her cigarettes out away from her face, forgetting them in her hands until there was nothing but ash. She liked to play dress-up with her old school-teaching clothes.

Grandad kept his marbles but had had a heart attack the month before his 60th birthday. Now he walked around the ranch aimlessly, shirtless, with a zipper-scar on his chest. He remained, by his own admission, a thoroughgoing pussy hound.

Deacon believed that he was on his way to discovering the truth about Grandad, like finding a hard, sweet seed at the center of a sour fruit. *No kin, no care.* It was something his father used to say, though he had never really understood it.

Deacon looked at the Unruhs with occasional disgust. They disappointed him. He was a teenager, and he had hoped to stay on with them at the ranch. Now the ranch was a joke. They called themselves ranchers long after the ranch had been reduced to skeletal sheep and blooming weeds.

Deacon began to think about college as a way out. He didn't really understand what it would mean for him, or what it would enable him do, if anything. Late at night, Deacon read his textbooks, brushing his blond bangs from his eyes, and he listened to his mother's drunken sleep-talk in the next room, dreaming the accident of his birth. "Goddamn Jack," she'd slur. "I'm pregnant, you fucker."

One day Deacon landed a job interview, and Grandad agreed to lend him his pick-up. Grandad hadn't been allowed to drive for some time. Doctor's orders.

It was the first time the truck had been started in weeks, and it choked to life, expelling a family of tiny field mice from the muffler. Standing in a cloud of exhaust, Grandad stared down at the mice, their brown fur stained with oily condensation. The mice trembled like homunculi in the yellow grass, stunned. He laughed and gently kicked them out of the way so Deacon could throw the truck in reverse before it died.

"Better light out, boy," he said, secretly adjusting himself through his pocket. With his other hand, he waved goodbye.

Deacon drove slowly to his interview, not sure what to expect.

The advertisement had been almost buried in the paper, for it was spring, and there were chicks and ducklings listed for Easter. *I Need A House Cleaner. Would prefer all-natural products.*

"That's for girls," Mrs. Unruh had said, knitting her brows.

"Doesn't say nothing about girls or boys," Deacon said. "Can't hurt to call."

Mrs. Unruh tilted her face, confused. "But you can get a job right now, on the ranches," she said. To her, Deacon was a puddle of strange ideas.

"Not on *your* ranch," he said. "I need to save money for college. If I want a career," Deacon pointed at the television. A show was playing with high-powered lawyers in business suits. The lawyers stood and argued outside on marble steps for what seemed like forever.

Mrs. Unruh stared at the men in suits. By their side were women with briefcases. The kind of women Grandad called femi-nazis, the kind he said needed a good roll behind the barn.

Mrs. Unruh's white-blond hair was pulled back into a chignon. She was playing dress-up again. "Wanna come look at my purses?" she asked.

"I gotta get home and make my mom some dinner. Ask Grandad when he gets back if I can use his truck, 'kay?"

She looked at him for a moment, and then her frail hand wandered toward his cheek. He had the first traces of stubble, like the legs of a caterpillar.

"Po, po, pitiful thing. How'd you get to be so pitiful?" she asked.

∗

Turned out the dirty house belonged to Dr. Scully, the heart doctor.

It was the first time Deacon had ever been inside a rich person's house. He tried not to stare at the artful spiral of a wine rack, or the gold enameled Buddhas everywhere, or the skylights. He made a point of wiping his feet thoroughly on a mat that read Home Is Where Your Ohm Is. Though the house was a mansion and full of expensive-looking knick-knacks, it was furnished with second-hand furniture, ugly futons and stained chairs.

During the interview, Deacon sat at the Scullys' kitchen table, which glittered like snow. Melodee Buttress-Scully, the wife of the doctor who operated on Grandad, explained that it was made of recycled glass from wine bottles all over the world. Deacon thought about his mother passed out on the brown couch after work, her lips stained grape-purple.

"A male house cleaner must be pretty controversial in such a provincial town," Mrs. Buttress-Scully said, turning her head from side to side as if addressing an unseen audience.

"I dunno," Deacon said, noticing a framed picture on the wall with a man suspended by a bungee cord in a canyon. He wondered if it was Dr. Scully. "I guess it's not that different from being a janitor." He didn't know what else to say. He was about to mention his plan to save for college, when she said:

"Van and I pride ourselves on being progressive in all areas of our life. Do you know what that means—progressive?"

Melodee Buttress-Scully and her husband were not like anyone Deacon had ever met. They had lived everywhere, never one place for long, and Deacon had the sense that they didn't intend to stay in Comanche very long either. During the interview, Melodee Buttress-Scully seemed distracted, as if she was running late, and her coarse black hair rose up in the dry air. It seemed as if she might have to move again by the afternoon.

She explained what she wanted of Deacon, that she was very, very busy, and as she described her high standards, she lifted a thin arm above her head. She wanted him to pay attention to the smallest things. She wanted him to take a Q-tip to the places between the numbers on the clock.

Deacon nodded, barely saying a word.

"And I will check after you," Melodee Buttress-Scully said, with a tone that was serious but still polite. "I'll run my fingers along the baseboards."

"I understand," Deacon said.

•

When he got back to the trailer, he found his mother smoking something that made the house smell of beef jerky. She was still in her work blouse, though it was open at the neck, revealing a small patch of freckled skin. "Where you been all day, Deac?"

"At school. Then the job interview. I took Grandad's truck."

She rolled over on the couch, wrinkling her clothes. A gray cloud of jerky smoke hung down over her. "You know I don't like you hanging around that old pervert."

Deacon started pulling things out of the refrigerator and pantry, one by one. An onion. A bag of egg noodles. Chocolate milk.

"Don't worry about him, he just wants people to think he's an ignoramus. He's really an *old soul*," Deacon said, using a term he had heard his English teacher say. He liked it, even though he didn't completely understand what it meant. "How was work?"

Deacon's mother laughed, her teeth dark. "You said something about a job?"

"It's a cleaning job I found in the paper. I interviewed with Dr. Scully's wife after school, and I guess I'm hired."

"Fucking rich people," Deacon's mother said. "Can't even clean their own houses. You want me to make some dinner?"

"I'm making it. Don't trouble yourself." He glared at his mother, folded over like a pile of dirty clothes.

"Call your aunts before you do that. Tell them about the job. They'll be proud of you, like I'm proud of you."

She was always telling Deacon she was proud of him for doing the littlest things, for putting his shoes on in the morning. Deacon's Aunt Jeanette once told him that his mother had been convinced that Deacon would be born retarded because she couldn't stop drinking wine boxes during the pregnancy, even though she had been warned to quit. Maybe, Deacon thought, that was why she was so proud when he could even breathe or take a shit.

As he made powdered mac n'cheese, Deacon cradled the phone against his shoulder and called his Aunt. His mother was right. Aunt Jeanette was proud. Aunt Jeanette said she'd hang up and call the other aunts.

When the family matriarchs heard that Deacon had taken a job as a cleaning person, they were pleased and nodded sagely, their small heads rolling like grouse eggs. Though they universally acknowledged his mother to be a mess, they figured there was still hope for him. A job was a job. Frankly, they said, they were just grateful he hadn't driven off with his father and that Indian.

Deacon started the next day. He took Grandad's truck again, and Grandad waved goodbye and shouted at him as he drove off. "They don't make you wear an apron, do they?"

Deacon felt no remorse asking Grandad for the use of his truck, or for money, not that there was much of that anymore. Grandad felt guilty for Deacon's pitiable life, and being a whip-smart boy of the prairie, Deacon exploited Grandad's guilt. Also he had been eyewitness to Grandad putting his tongue down a sixteen-year-old girl's throat the summer before. The Gomez family only spared Grandad's cheek bones because his wife rented them the trailer, and because Deacon—now tall enough to look at least mildly threatening—offered to intervene. After the Gomezes left, kicking up a cloud of dust and threats to crush Grandad's balls with their monster truck, Grandad patted Deacon on the shoulder.

"You really saved me."

"Don't forget it," Deacon said, sounding a little like his father.

That morning when he got to work, Deacon learned that the Buttress-Scullys had children. They were all different colors—a black boy, a brown girl, and a white boy. The children were restless, beginning games and puzzles in brief bursts of activity while breathing heavily. Sometimes they spun in rapid circles, their bony arms outstretched like fan blades, and shouted the names for animals in English and French until the two names became almost indistinguishable. Then they'd fall to the carpet laughing, vomiting up frothy saliva from their lips. With each game, they focused themselves completely with piercing concentration, only to abandon their endeavors abruptly with a barely a flinch.

Deacon was frightened of them. He hadn't spent much time around small children. There were Grandad's farm animals, but it wasn't the same. There were rules with them, like the horses you had to approach from the side, leaving them ample room to move. But these children were smarter and therefore more unpredictable.

The white boy, Torrance, ran up to Deacon when he was dusting and shoved him in the stomach.

Melodee Buttress-Scully, who sat on the futon reading a story in Spanish to the brown girl, said "Boys will be boys." She ran her fingers nervously through her frizzy hair. "I'm sure you remember from your own childhood."

Deacon thought of crawling on the carpet, being a pawn for his mother.

"Actually, my dad would have tanned me pink," he lied. It felt good.

Mrs. Buttress-Scully shrugged. "I don't believe in corporal punishment. Van and I believe you should talk to and treat children like people." She looked out the window at the mountains. "Of course I realize that's not how everyone was raised."

"That's okay," Deacon said, and went back to dusting. He cautiously observed the children while carrying out the remaining tasks of the day.

⁂

"How was it?" Grandad asked when he came home.

"It was a job." Deacon threw him his keys. "I don't see how it's going to pay enough for college. And the kids are weird. Paloma, Torrance, and Kwezi."

"Kwezi? That doctor cut open my chest, he didn't look foreign."

"I think they're adopted," Deacon said, going in to wash his hands.

"Or two of them, at least. Your truck needs work, old man," he shouted over his shoulder.

"You just call me old?" Grandad asked, thrusting out his damaged chest. "Punk."

*

Melodee Buttress-Scully was too different for Comanche. She ran fourteen miles every morning, pushing Kwezi in a stroller the whole way. She gave herself beet juice enemas. After dipping her fingers in olive oil, she stood in front of the mirror and smeared her fingertips down the length of each strand of hair, letting the loose hairs fall to the bathroom floor where Deacon knelt, scrubbing the base of the toilet. Sometimes Mrs. Buttress-Scully rolled out a little mat in a patch of afternoon sunlight on the carpet, and bent her back into octagons.

Her greatest passion was her involvement in an organization called *Leche Internacional,* an operation celebrating the joys of breastfeeding. Deacon gleaned most of the information about *Leche Internacional* from papers on the Scullys' desk, which he frequently, clandestinely, flipped through hoping to see pictures of breasts. He listened as Mrs. Buttress-Scully took phone calls in her "office" regarding the Comanche start-up branch she was attempting, which mainly seemed to consist of women in Sheridan. She spearheaded an effort to ship the frozen breast milk of American women to Bhutan.

She didn't seem to care for Deacon. "You could have done a better job in the kitchen," she'd say, her bony fingers pinching at her waist. When she made lunch—usually recipes from back issues of a health food magazine that he had to stack neatly on the counter—she never offered Deacon anything. If people came to visit Melodee Buttress-Scully, as they sometimes did, usually people Deacon had never seen around town, she gestured to him with a degree of embarrassment, as if he were an unfortunate water stain on the ceiling, but did not introduce him.

*

One day as he was windexing the living room window, Deacon noticed a man on a skinny racing bike wending up the hill to the house. The bike was the gunmetal color of a cattle prod, and the bicyclist wore a serious black helmet with green stripes bisecting it. Dr. Van Scully. Deacon had been working for the Scullys over a month and had never met him.

Dr. Scully was the bungee jumper from the picture. He was probably in his forties, Deacon figured, but even from within his spandex biker's suit, his muscles protruded in shiny, rubbery waves. In the absent-minded manner of ritual, Dr. Scully bowed at the gold-plated Buddha squatting near the front door before coming in.

Dr. Scully walked through the house with his hand extended. "You must be the wunderkind. What did we ever do before you came?"

Deacon put down his dust rag to shake the doctor's hand. "Nice to meet you."

"Ah, so formal!" The doctor boomed genially. "I feel like I've known you forever, everything Melodee says about you."

What had Mrs. Buttress-Scully said about him? Deacon couldn't imagine what she'd tell Dr. Scully, except maybe that he sometimes skipped the top wine bottle when dusting, but that was because he couldn't reach it and the Scullys didn't own a ladder. He scrambled for some kind of response but was distracted by the image of Dr. Scully with his helmet still on. His head looked like a sideways almond.

"Hey. You're a godsend, I'm telling you. She was going crazy before, with the children, balancing all her international work, trying to hold things together here. I'm sure you can imagine. You probably wish you had someone to clean your own house, huh?" He laughed raucously, causing the Tibetan prayer flags to flutter in the doorway.

Deacon tried to laugh back. He tried to imagine the doctor stitching closed Grandad's chest, sealing up his well-worn heart.

Dr. Scully pulled a lunch bag out of the refrigerator. "Well, I've gotta run back to the office, but I'm glad to finally meet you. Thanks for holding down the fort."

"Van?" Mrs. Buttress-Scully had been doing one of her detox soaks in the upstairs bathroom. Deacon always avoided the upstairs when she was there, as she had the habit of walking naked from her bedroom to the bath.

"Who else?" The doctor cheerfully rummaged through some papers on the kitchen counter.

"Are you staying?" She descended the stairs, pulling closed her green silk robe. In a dramatic motion, she crossed the room and embraced Dr. Scully, who kissed her open-mouthed while holding her face.

Deacon, deeply embarrassed—he had never even seen his own parents kiss—looked away, but not before glimpsing the inside edge of Mrs. Buttress-Scully's small breast as her robe stretched open.

"I was going to go for a run, if you could watch the children for a while," she murmured into his mouth.

Dr. Scully looked up, surprised. "I'm due back at the office." He turned toward Deacon. "But I'm sure our good friend could watch them for an hour or so. Those buggers aren't too much of a handful."

From Paloma's bedroom came a crashing sound, and Kwezi appeared in the doorway, staring at his parents with huge ghost-eyes. Deacon forced himself to nod and smile fakely at Kwezi, all the while realizing that Dr. Scully either didn't know or had forgotten his name.

Though the afternoon passed without incident, Deacon drove home with a bad feeling. Bad omen. Like the kind his mother claimed to get just before her period. Her whole body, she'd say, like chicken wire in the wind.

Grandad and Mrs. Unruh announced they were leaving. They had planned on settling in Seattle, but after they determined their only sur-viving relatives were less than enthusiastic about taking them in, they decided to move to Florence, Oregon, where apartments were relatively cheap and the weather decent, rain notwithstanding. Grandad knew someone there who could get him a Parks & Recreation job and someone who could keep an eye on Mary-Beth, who had begun to leave the door unlocked. In late spring, they sold all the trailers to a rental corporation called WestSky and the ranch with the starving sheep to a couple from Los Angeles.

"Can't you wait til summer?" Deacon asked. "At least then I wouldn't have school, and I could help you move. I could drive with you."

"We don't need no help. There ain't nothing to be moved," Grandad said matter-of-factly, taking off his shirt. His scar had become brown and scabby. It was hot for April, and Grandad and Deacon dragged the hose out to fill up the water buckets. "Besides, you can come visit when you get done. Before college. They got them huge sand dunes there, people ride 'em with dune buggies and skateboards and all."

Deacon didn't have it in him to tell Grandad he hadn't even applied for college.

In the window, Mrs. Unruh stared out at him, one hand shielding her brow. Her eyes were nearly white with cataracts. She waved at him once with one of her patent leather purses. Deacon was surprised to have to swallow something down in his throat.

"You think you'd like to run them dunes like that, boy?" Grandad asked, yanking hard on the hose.

"How the hell do you skateboard on sand?" Deacon wondered, pulling one of the sheep down into a squat against his legs. Grandad aimed the hose at the sheep's mouth, but it turned its head trying to avoid the water. Against his shins, he could feel the sheep's spine.

"Fuck if I know," Grandad said.

After they finished with the sheep, Grandad dropped Deacon off back at his mother's trailer.

It was scorching hot, and Deacon went from room to room, opening the windows. Each one was limned with black mildew.

His mother had acquired a boyfriend of one month, a man from work named Nave Goodall. He was one of her two bosses at the shady utility company. He had a habit of driving his car through the small patch of grass Mrs. Unruh had seeded years ago in the center of the trailer park, a square of green in the midst of yellow prairie grass and gravel, and his tires left ugly dirt tracks where the grass had been.

When Deacon opened the door to his mother's bedroom and found her pinned beneath Nave Goodall, his sweaty ass bouncing above her bed like a rubber kickball, he was not surprised. Nave Goodall, however, stopped in mid-air, and Deacon's mother craned her head from under his ruddy shoulder.

"What is it, Deac? You want me to make some dinner?"

"Nah. I just wanted to tell you Grandad and Mrs. Unruh are moving to Oregon. Somebody else is going to be renting us the trailer from now on. Some corporation. They're raising the rent two hundred bucks."

Nave Goodall gently lowered himself back down on Deacon's mother.

Deacon's mother laughed, her purple lips crinkling. "Fucking old pervert, Unruh," she said. "How am I supposed to afford that?"

Deacon pulled the door closed behind him. "I'll go see if there's anything in the fridge for dinner."

"Seriously," Deacon's mother said into Nave Goodall's shoulder. "How the fuck am I supposed to afford that?"

*

At school, Deacon was barely there, just counting the days until the end of the year. Sometimes it felt like he really was invisible. He could go a whole day without a single person speaking to him. No one even made the horse shit jokes about him anymore.

At work, his responsibilities grew, though he suffered less super-
vision. The doctor's wife disappeared for hours at a time, and Deacon
was asked to listen out for the children during their afternoon naps. He
prayed that they wouldn't wake up; he wouldn't know what to do if they
did.

When she was home, Mrs. Buttress-Scully had little patience for Deacon. Her irritation seemed worse as the weather grew warmer, when it
became too hot to jog and her hair frizzed up in the desert heat. "Do you
have to do that?" she'd carp when he ran the vacuum during her stretch-
ing sessions.

Once, when he yelled at Torrance for pulling cat turds out of the litter
box, she grabbed his wrist hard. "*You aren't allowed to discipline him.*"

"I wasn't going to touch him," Deacon said, reddening. "You saw him.
He was getting his hands in cat shit."

He was sure in that moment that she would fire him, cut him a check
for the rest of the day's work and let him go. Instead she slowly released
her grip like she was coming awake, leaving the mark of her fingers on
his skin.

Deacon told himself he didn't care. He didn't want any part of her,
with her honey hair treatments that clogged the tub or her new ability to
place her legs behind her head while using prayer hands; though truth
be told, he sometimes did think of her instead of girls at school when he
touched himself late at night. He didn't understand how it was that he
could be aroused by a woman he didn't even find all that attractive, with
her skinny fingers and flexible legs—but just the same, when he came
staring at the wood paneling in his bedroom, it was her small breast he
thought of.

Still, she was a bitch, as Grandad had always said.

*

Deacon developed a technique of cleaning several rooms at once, allowing him to move freely to a different room if Mrs. Buttress-Scully came
in. He worked diligently and quickly in the hopes of being released early.
Unfortunately, with the children running around, Deacon's work was
frequently undone by the end of the day, and he found himself staying
later, ultimately subjected to Dr. Scully's idle chitchat when he biked back
home, energized from a day of cutting open people's hearts.

More and more, Deacon thought about quitting, now that it was clear
he couldn't afford college. But he knew his mother would have to forfeit

the trailer if he did. Despite the fucking, Nave Goodall wouldn't give her a raise.

Sometimes when he came home from school and work, he'd stand around in the empty lot where Mary-Beth Unruh's trailer used to be. The trailer itself had been moved to the edge of the park, back where the Mexicans lived, to make room for a new trailer office that the WestSky people were going to build. Once or twice, a man in a white shirt with a notebook had come to look around, taking measurements, bringing other men who took more measurements. Deacon avoided them, but he heard his mother talking to the man in a loud voice, and then later, in a strange, desperate voice, fingering the open button on her work blouse. Since WestSky had taken over, she had upgraded to nearly two boxes of wine a night.

Deacon stood in the empty square, kicking at the gravel. He thought about Grandad in Oregon, getting rained on, and Mrs. Unruh's cloudy eyes looking out at the sea. Deacon wondered if they ever missed Comanche. He kicked harder, deeper, and imagined he was rattling poor dead Martha the Terrible's chains.

•

Just before school let out, Deacon slipped in Melodee Buttress-Scully's personal lubricant and nearly cracked his skull open on the imported Greek marble floor. He landed with his head at an awkward angle behind the toilet, where there was more lubricant, and also the greenish stain of old urine from Dr. Scully's prostate. He lay there gathering his wits for several minutes until it became clear that no one was home, and even if they had been, they would not have concerned themselves with him.

He finished cleaning the remainder of the upstairs, gently picking up the Scullys' things. Dr. Scully's palm tree decorated boxer shorts, their meditation manuals, wooden statues from their travels, and books about Gandhi, about the Donner party, stacked next to pictures of their children. Kwezi somewhere in what looked like Africa, Paloma in a swimming pool at SeaWorld, flanked by killer whales.

Deacon considered how little time it had taken for what once seemed so exotic and strange to him to become commonplace and boring. The doctor who stuck his fist into people's chests. The woman who had never breastfed a child, shipping milk around the world. Would his life have been different had he been given clean milk, untainted by cheap wine?

Around the house, he had begun to notice change-of-address forms. There was talk of Dr. Van Scully taking a fellowship in Canada, of Mrs. Buttress-Scully joining The Yoga Institute of Vancouver, raising the children among a bilingual people. The Scullys would move on soon, taking their children with them—maybe even adding to their brood—to the next town where they would include a small cowboy statue for Comanche, WY on their shelf of curiosities. Deacon wondered if they would even remember him in a year's time, that strange local boy who cleaned their house.

He had the sudden urge to smash their Buddhas, to carve his name into all of their belongings.

•

At the end of summer, after school was over and after he had quit the Scullys with a firm but polite letter, Deacon Friddle took the Greyhound from Sheridan to Oregon to visit Grandad. His mother didn't mind. It meant an uninterrupted week with Nave Goodall.

Deacon had never been more than a hundred miles away from Comanche in his entire life. He was privileged with the window seat, his only company a businessman who slept with his mouth open for almost the duration of the journey. Watching the scenery change as the bus carved its way through mountain passes, the rolling yellow hills soon poked through with pines, and eventually the white, misty blankness of the coast, Deacon was thrilled. His blood rose to his face and seemed to set his pompadour ablaze.

Finally, there was the Pacific Ocean, crashing with a violence he could not look away from.

Grandad met him up on the dunes. He had rented him a board. "Turns out they don't need wheels," he said, smacking Deacon on the back. He stood back and laughed as Deacon made an honest effort to surf his way down an enormous, rock-hard dune, ending up flat on his face with a mouth full of sand.

Afterward, Grandad took Deacon out for lunch at a crab shack. Grandad's hair and beard had gone completely white, and his hands shook a little when he went to break off the crab legs. Grandad asked after Deacon's mother. Deacon shrugged, as if to say, more of the same.

"Some people aren't meant to be parents," Grandad said sadly. His shirt was unbuttoned at the neck, and his skin was dark, darker even than it had been back at the ranch. The zipper scar alone was white as abalone.

"How do *you* know?" Deacon asked. "You never had any kids. You're not even a real Grandad."

Grandad waved his hand dismissively. "She shoulda never done it if she weren't gonna do it right. Drinking and lazing around like that." He shook his head and sighed, making a small whistling sound as he exhaled. "Ended up treating you something pitiful."

"I don't want to talk about her," Deacon said. "I want to hear about you."

So Grandad told him about his life, which had mostly been good, with some bad spread in between. The Parks & Recreation job wasn't much of anything, basically cleaning public toilets and picking up trash. But there was one great part: Every so often a whale would wash up on shore. Usually a fin whale, sometimes a blue. There was no way to get rid of them once they died, and they'd stink up the beach for tourists if they weren't disposed of. Grandad's job was to pack them with dynamite and blow them up.

"Like goddamn Fourth of July!" He grinned. "You should see it."

Grandad talked and talked. Mrs. Unruh had died. Grandad said the worst part was how confused she got at the end, talking about her imaginary children. "She mentioned you a lot. I think she somehow got in her head you were hers," he said. But he was not too grief-stricken; he had convinced himself it was for the best. "She's out of her suffering. Doesn't have to worry about scoundrels like me." What he felt most bad about was the fact he couldn't bury her with the dog back in Comanche.

Deacon stayed with Grandad for five days. Grandad showed him a good time, doing his best to erase the previous pitiable eighteen years of Deacon Friddle's life. They walked along the shore, and Grandad took him up the dunes near the fancy houses, where there were remnants of gray-white blubber from one of his recent whale explosions. It glittered on the grass.

On the last day they went to the Oregon Coast Aquarium, where they observed the fragile movements of jellyfish and the stalking, stiff-legged gait of giant crabs, and Grandad made a joke about butter.

They watched a young, attractive girl diving in a tank with small sharks, cleaning the walls of a fake coral reef with a toothbrush. Every now and then a nurse shark would swim up behind her, and she'd turn around and take stock of it.

"That one's sure pretty to look at," Grandad said. "Must be a pistol to take a job like that."

"Shut up, pervert." Deacon said.

The diver continued swimming through the reef. Her red hair—buffeted by the mechanically engineered currents—rippled out from her mask.

Deacon stared at her slender body as she scrubbed at the fuzzy algae. Suddenly she looked up at him and waved.

Continuity in Filmmaking

Geoffrey has been a good helpmate and lover in our home, as well as a renaissance man at work, but he cannot be in two places simultaneously. For proof of this, I can point to the empty side of our bed, or to the absence of his dun-colored hairs on the pillow, or to the remarkably clear water in the bottom of the toilet bowl. When he arrives home, Geoffrey reclines on the bed to remove his shoes, sending a fine rain of dirt from his soles to the bedspread. Then he takes a leak first thing after and doesn't flush the mellow yellows.

The specificity of these details proves that I am not lying, or at least that it is unlikely that I am lying. They say that in a court of law, during testimony, a jury should be vigilant about the specificity of details. A vague story with a dearth of details marks the storyteller as a liar. Of course, it is possible that I am confused or mistaken. I was in a car accident six months ago, my head smashed into the windshield. Two men flanked by three women and one additional man operated on me for four hours; little fragments of glass were removed from my brain. When I woke in the hospital, part of my forehead was dented in like a doll's head. I lost some memories, that's what Geoffrey says. And sometimes when I'm talking to him, I realize he's actually one of his sport jackets or a shadow or the shower curtain. So I'm not saying that I'm faultless.

But here, now: no hair, no dirt, no piss. The lack of these things proves that Geoffrey isn't here.

Geoffrey is training Nimrod, a bull terrier, for a half hour sitcom called *Man's Best Friend*. He is a dog trainer, though he calls himself a "people trainer." Training dogs for the world's entertainment is his life's purpose.

In the script it says that Nimrod, playing a bull terrier named Louie, is supposed to grab a hot dog from the hand of a three-year-old boy. The boy's name I don't know. A laugh track will play like a chorus of lunatics as the child and his mother, an actress who calls herself Patricia Duvae Lovell, chuckle with good humor. The camera will frame Nimrod's jowls as he chews the hot dog with an impish canine *joie de vivre*.

Things are not going as planned. The dog is frozen on the steps, a decade of arthritis locking his hips.

"Come on, Nimrod," Geoffrey says. "Take it. Take it?"

This is as good a time as any to mention that I don't give a crap about this show. I watched it in the hospital when nothing else was on, and it actually made me feel sick. It's a terrible show, the kind that no one watches and is scheduled on Saturday nights when everyone is out drinking, and anyway, none of it matters because Geoffrey is supposed to be here, in our house, and not there, at the studio. He's supposed to get his car out of my garage and then his things out of my house, or he's supposed to grab my shoulders and shake me like a snow globe until both of us resemble what we were before. Either way, we need to talk and reconcile and be mature and do the things that adults do, and we can't do any of those things when one of us is somewhere else.

A treat, moistened with the sweat of his palm, is inches away from Nimrod's nose. Geoffrey will smell like bacon and bull penis for the rest of the day.

"Take it?"

Nimrod descends the final two steps.

"This is when they look at you like God," Geoffrey likes to say. With a quick flick of his fingers, he sends the dog, entranced, to the child, and then to the hot dog. Mission accomplished.

It's remarkable what some people get paid for. Before the accident, I was paid to fetch things for studio heads and ingénues, for anyone who happened to be present on any given day of the shoot. I met Geoffrey on a commercial for canine herbal supplements, with a collie pulling an amputee. We bonded over a box of flea dip. I was the courier of ten varieties of latte. Spec scripts. I drove people whose names I didn't know to plastic surgeons and, afterwards, I helped them out of the secret back doors of buildings, swathed in hoods and designer bandages. I brought five or six magazines to read while they were under the knife, but I always timed it perfectly based on the procedure, so they didn't know how unambitiously I passed the time.

I was so good, I could have done my job and Geoffrey's combined. I could've trained Geoffrey to take treats, to mouth processed meat from the fist of a toddler. Even now, I can remember the entire cast and crew of *Man's Best Friend,* down to the craft service guy and his wife and their white kid with a retro afro. How come I can remember these useless things? I lose pens and buttons and Geoffrey's ex-wife's name, his kid's name, even my name sometimes, but I remember everything about Geoffrey's day-to-day dealings with dogs and Hollywood assholes.

Geoffrey trains six dogs: Marvin the mutt, Waldo the collie, Kibbles the bulldog, Yoda the Boston terrier, Miss Pebbles the Brussels Griffon, and Nimrod. They all belong to other people, but they spend more time with Geoffrey than they do with their owners. In total, Geoffrey works with five studio suits: Mr. Bunton, Mr. Graves, Mr. Khandakhor, Ms. Sterling, and Mr. Lowenstein. Geoffrey belongs to me, but he spends more time with the suits than he does with his owner.

In his absence, the lack of him has come to resemble him more than the actual him. His mother's in a nursing home and has a photograph of him on her wall above a bedpan. It's from when he ran track in college. It doesn't look at all like him now that he's softened and thickened and thinned out, but how would she know? As far as I can tell, he hasn't called his mother in months, but luckily she probably doesn't remember that. We're all the same, dented heads or not.

Right about now, Geoffrey and Nimrod have finished the scene. It's a wrap, which means that a girl named Meggie Barclay is on her knees in front of Geoffrey taking photographs of Nimrod. Nimrod's collar. Close-ups of his paws, the direction his fur's been brushed. Even the type of hot dog.

They call this "continuity in filmmaking." Meggie Barclay is the person in charge of maintaining continuity, so that if they have to shoot the scene over again tomorrow, Nimrod will look exactly the same. Everything will be seamless, and the audience won't know the same scene was shot over the course of many days. I doubt people would care, but this is an important part of filmmaking, or so Meggie Barclay says. For some reason, Geoffrey holds her in high regard, as he does with most of these Hollywood power bitches. When she talks, she moves her nostrils, which I have always considered a sign of a person coming unhinged. Probably because she has to remember so much, so many details, the same day every day, forever.

It is an impossible feat to remember a whole person, the groove under his nose or his vinyl, car-seat smell. Looking at his dusty Hemingway collection helps. I used to read Hemingway, but I can't remember any of his books now. Weren't all the men amnesiacs? Hadn't they all been shot in the head?

I take all of Geoffrey's shoes out of the closet and arrange them in patterns across the floor. It seems they're all going somewhere. Once, Geoffrey and I took ballroom dancing lessons with a woman named Maria. She had a thick accent, something like a Spanish villainess. We couldn't understand a thing she said, just "Deep!" for dip, and "Bank!" for back, but that was okay because she had these little shoes painted on the floor, and really you just had to match your feet up with them to master the steps.

I point Geoffrey's eighty dollar beach loafers toward the front door. They're probably going to see Patricia Duvae Lovell or someone similarly fake and whorish. Who was that girl, the one they hired to help him wrangle the dogs and block scenes. A grip? A second assistant boom? He liked her because she did some bullshit cliché thing like raising chickens on her roof. Or roosters.

I'm not jealous, or paranoid. I don't think Geoffrey would cheat. I just think he's friendly with everyone, which is a truly horrible character trait.

In the hospital, Geoffrey sat by my bed for a week. Then he went back to work. It wasn't that he was heartless, exactly. They were shooting a pilot called *Braver Than Brave,* featuring a Puli named Nuba. I was driving Nuba to the Studio to meet Geoffrey when I had my accident. A tour bus blew a tire and slid across six lanes of traffic, like in a bad Bruce Willis movie. I don't remember anything about it, just a cracking sound, and then waking up in the hospital to Geoffrey's face, that little constellation of moles down his neck. When I asked him what happened, he said Nuba had gone through the windshield. Nuba was dead. I asked him over and over how it was that my head just smashed the thick glass but didn't go through, yet Nuba flew into the air like a black mop. "Seatbelt," Geoffrey said. "Seatbelt." I don't think Geoffrey has forgiven me.

They ended up filming *Braver Than Brave* with Marvin the mutt, who really was smarter anyway.

His last message is there somewhere on the phone. He's talking in his "calm voice," what he uses to soothe Nimrod when he gets all pissy from the fourteen hours of shooting situation comedies. "Now, Nimrod? Go to your place," he's always saying when Nimrod gets that look in his eye and curls his top lip under like an eighty-year-old woman.

He says something about noon. *Unable. Hon.* He is busy. He is not cre-
ative. At least take a rain check from the elevator where you delivered a
baby. Let there have been a diabetic stretched out on the floor, weak head
in your lap.

I take all his blazers and position them on the bed like victims of a
crime. "Guess you didn't see it coming," I say, my voice low like a detec-
tive's. "Maybe you should've paid better attention to the company you
keep." I link the sleeves of three sport jackets until they look like Hands
Across America, or a family.

When the phone rings, I jump and grab at his fallen jackets.

"Listen, it's a fucking mess," he says. "I can't come." He fades in and
out. "You don't have rags and bandages, do you?"

"What the hell happened?"

"It was an accident."

"You mean . . . like a bus in a pile-up? My kind of accident?" Perhaps
the tour bus was going fast enough to slide through the space-time con-
tinuum, cutting down people over the course of a year, still taking them
down, a runaway death machine.

"Don't start," he grumbles. "Fucking Nimrod bit me."

"He bit you. Why? He's ancient."

"How do I know why? He wanted the goddamn hot dog. Fuck it, I
can't come home. I'm going over to Meggie's now."

"I want you to come here."

"I'm probably going to have to get a rabies shot. I'm bleeding."

It sounds like a bad talk show, but he really has been distant since the
accident. He says it's my moods, but I think it's something else entirely.
Sometimes I laugh hysterically for no real reason. Last week he came in
when I was in the shower and I didn't recognize his voice so I started
screaming and begged him to leave and not kill me. He stopped sleeping
in the bed with me when I'd wake up convinced my head was still dented
in, or part of it missing, and I'd grab his fingers and make him touch my
scalp.

We were supposed to meet after work last night at the Golf Pub down
the block. He hates when I call it the "Golf Pub." It's the "Pebble Beach
Pub," he says. The bar at the pub is covered in glass, and under the glass
there are fifty-three Titleist golf balls, plus autographed photographs of
golfers. Last night, I recognized the one with the alcohol problem. He has
a red face. Geoffrey didn't come, so I sat around drinking for a couple of
hours. I asked the bartender if I could touch his balls. "You fucking crazy,
you know that?" he asked, and we both laughed until he finally stopped.

Nimrod's getting old. He's not the cash cow, or cash dog, he used to be. Sometimes he pukes or shits in the car on the way to auditions and Geoffrey has to clean up on the side of the 405. The fucking traffic nearly shears the door off. "I should have him sire pups," he's always saying. "Nimrod's genes are solid." He's still got the Brussels Griffon at least. Everyone who wants a cutesy wootsy little girl dog wants the Brussels Griffon. He's made a lot off her and she's still young, still has those eyes that glitter and don't look burnt out from jumping around too many soundstages.

Geoffrey almost never talks about his son, but he gets emotional about his dogs. He still carries a photo of Nuba in his wallet, even though she wasn't even his dog. "When you train a dog," he says, "you really get inside its head." I want him to get inside my head and tell me what it looks like. What's the damage.

I go out and sit in his car. I'm not allowed to drive yet, so I'll close my eyes and pretend I'm waiting for Geoffrey to return from a secret facelift. It smells like Nimrod and dog piss. There's dog fur or pubic hair on the passenger seat, some kinky brindled hairs that float through the air with the windows down. I try re-lighting all his cigarette butts in the ashtray, sucking down what he's left behind. Sometimes I bring them inside the house with me and hide them in my pillowcase.

Now that I think of it, when we were first dating, sometimes he didn't show. There was "car in the shop" and twice "paperwork." What kind of fucking paperwork does a dog trainer have? Sometimes he cancelled after I left the house. I didn't know he wasn't coming until I got home and found him among my voicemail. Even now, it is pleasant just to drink a glass of wine and eat part of a chicken while listening to his voice.

Usually by now he's done for the day and on his way to Nimrod's owners' house. They live deep in Topanga Canyon. "It's lucky," Geoffrey says, "that coyotes didn't take Nimrod away." Once while the owners were jogging with him, Nimrod got grabbed. Nimrod was so heavy, so dense and thick, the coyote just carried him from one place to another, dropping him behind the juniper and picking him up again. It couldn't really get its mouth around him. Finally the owners came and beat off the coyote with sticks. I laughed when Geoffrey told me that story. "I was just a coyote for the studio heads," I said. "And for you. From one place to another."

Over the last two months, as part of my therapy, Geoffrey has to drive me to Neuro-Spinal Rehab. I have to sit in a room while a woman who sometimes looks like Meggie Barclay and sometimes looks like just another blond woman holds up a series of cards with illustrations on them. I'm supposed to identify each one and say the name out loud. Boat. Bear. Clown. It's harder than it looks. More often than not, it doesn't look like anything.

What *are* the details of his skin and hair? My testimony of what's happened to us would be thrown out in a court of law. I find myself forgetting him all the time, even when he's here. Even when he's inside me. *Wait, who are you again?* I want to ask, my nails digging into his hips. Writing things down doesn't help. Maybe it's because I'm always using the lack of details to prove his absence. Nothing equals nothing.

I remember he once said he hated all the Beatles except for George Harrison. He was proud of himself because he said most people loved John and Paul, and others loved Ringo because he was the quirky choice, but mostly, no one favored George. He liked to play his 45 of "Apple Scruffs" and dance around the room with me. He sometimes knocked over the lamp shaped like Buddha. When I play "Apple Scruffs" now, I just feel embarrassed. I don't want to knock anything over. I want to carry things around in my mouth, where they're safe.

I walk into the bathroom and take his electric razor out of my medicine cabinet. I like to jog my memory by flipping it over in my hand, taking its weight. Evidence.

I open it and sprinkle the flecks of hair in the porcelain sink. I remember the words "a soft bear" but I don't know why I remember them at this moment and not at any other. *Fuzzy Wuzzy was a bear, Fuzzy Wuzzy had no hair, Fuzzy Wuzzy wasn't very fuzzy, was he?* I want to call him my bear but he is busy training lions or maybe papers. With my index finger, I arrange the bits of hair into the shape of his face.

The specificity of my details suggests he might come home tonight. He'll be bleeding or clotting, wrapped in Meggie Barclay's healing bandages, or in a torn shower curtain. Meggie will stand in the doorway, holding her cards. Boat. Fuzzy bear. Clown.

"How ever do you remember it all?" I'll ask her. "I need reminders, little strings tied around my finger or stitches in my head. Mnemonic devices."

She'll shrug and walk around taking pictures so our dinner can last forever, all the details exactly the same.

He'll go into the bedroom and take off his shoes on the bed, sending down the dirt of his day. He'll walk over to his Hemingways and talk about plane crashes over Uganda and the importance of continuity in filmmaking.

"Stop moving around. You're getting blood all over the place."

"Goddamn Nimrod," Geoffrey will say. "Goddamn dog bit me."

"Why?" I'll ask, squeezing his bloody hand. "Show me. Where are the teeth marks?"

"How the fuck am I supposed to know why? Why does anything happen?"

"That's okay," I'll tell him. "Never mind. No one should be expected to remember all these things," I'll whisper, kissing him. "You're here, anyway." I'll hang up his blazer, take his papers, his jacket, and I will tell him not to worry, to remind me to take him into the bathroom later, by the sink, so I can be sure to show him his face.

Adwok, Pantokrator

When he still had a stubbled head, the boy Adwok attempted to subdue his temper, straining it through the veil of his afternoon prayers. He clenched his right foot, slightly deformed since birth, into the shape of a nautilus, releasing it one toe at a time. *Guide us on the straight path,* he said, setting his jaw, whispering his way into a groove of words. *The way of those on whom you have bestowed your grace, those whose portion is not wrath and who do not go astray.*

In another decade, after he had abandoned religion and the calluses on his knees had disappeared, he would wonder what all the fuss was about. The tired, half moon eyes, the endless rows of boys beside him, the pink soles of their feet marbled and cracked. All that time arching his body over a carpet when he could have been playing chess with Wiraj and Samir, if Wiraj and Samir weren't sprawled on the floor in Samir's father's basement watching month-old videos of the World Cup. Samir's father had money, had some business in oil, overseeing wildcatters in Jonglei. Samir's father didn't have religion. What he had was a sixty inch plasma TV.

But Adwok's father—a frail and uncertain dentist, permanently stooped from looking inside people—was a traditionalist, and Adwok was expected to behave in a serious, if not pious way, even if no one in his family, including his father, was particularly devout. His mother carped about covering her considerable length of hair and waxing her bikini line, the latter being an unwritten but nevertheless mandatory wifely duty, and his older brother David kept a black market wad of Euro sex magazines with names like *Friendly* and *Just Us!* on a high shelf in the closet. Given these transgressions, it seemed deeply unfair when Adwok first became acquainted with his father's sharp knuckles against his ear, and for nothing, really. For swearing, for not doing his homework. For raising the slightest objection to dropping everything come prayer time.

Parissa, nestled in their bed years hence, would say he didn't deserve it, despite the pleasure stewing in the corners of her small, purple mouth. "He beat ya ass," she crooned, spooning around him. "That's what all fathers do. They make and break you."

"What do you know about it?" he'd say, swatting her away.

"I know he fucking did that to ya foot." She had noticed it on the day they met, though initially she mistook it for a club foot. Sometimes she pulled back the sheets and stared at it like a dead rat in the bed.

"It wasn't from him, I told you. I got it being born."

"Doesn't matter," Parissa said. "He would have done it if he could of." She hated her parents, and his in absentia.

"Hey," Adwok said, resting his face between her breasts. "I'm not like that now. You don't *even* know. I had a *temper.*"

He hadn't enumerated all his misdeeds to her, just the stand-outs.

Powerless in his youth, Adwok had been angry, though he was no worse than the kids he deemed defectives at school. Those kids snuck cigarettes out of the deep drawers of their parents' dressers, set small fires in the blackened bowels of old trash cans near the Mac Nimir bridge. Adwok's was a more civilized temper. When his head came up from the floor, he sometimes locked eyes with the imams, who generally looked away. At two, he had kicked one of his myriad aunts, an old woman with arms like bat wings, in the shins. At five, he had cursed God in his mother's house. At ten, his portion was, in fact, a kind of middle-class, North Khartoum wrath. Unnameable, unplaceable, and flattened on all sides like a bale of hay, threatening to combust.

Still, though, he had noble aspirations, hopes of breeding his anger out like the turning over of old cells. James Bond, one of his and Samir's favorite cinema heroes, never showed rage. He was all calm comebacks and finesse. Perhaps Adwok's sons would be men who spoke in low voices and exercised elegant restraint. Maybe you could make and break them after all. He hoped, anyway.

◆

When Adwok was twelve, however, the family endured a series of ruptures.

After his mother was observed in a waiting room, sitting inappropriately close to an Omdurman civil servant, both there for flu shots, she became the subject of much gossip. Wiraj's mother claimed to have seen the two together on a day when Adwok's mother was gone from the house, having left allegedly to purchase gravel. That the gravel was for a makeshift driveway for a Volkswagon they hadn't even finished paying for made her errand all the more suspect. After a few days alone with her inner turmoil, Wiraj's mother decided it was her duty to inform the family of what everyone was talking about in a discreet, typed letter, with a carbon attached, quite quaintly.

Although the letter wasn't Wiraj's fault, Adwok stopped speaking to him, as did Samir out of childhood loyalty. Two weeks later, when Samir spread a rumor that Wiraj had a very bad case of head lice, Adwok said nothing to contradict him. For his part, Adwok spent the rest of the school year with a poisoned heart and a habit of puking before class. He lost six pounds. Somehow losing his best friend was worse than learning his mother had taken a lover.

Meanwhile, Adwok's father was quickly and easily granted a divorce. To himself, he admitted that questions about his wife's fidelity had always been there, free-ranging and worrisome. Still, despite the letter and the talk, he never really knew if she had been with the civil servant. He hadn't asked. To grapple with the complexities of their circumstances was too much for him, not the least because of his poor health, and he decided that probably his greatest mistake was getting married in the first place. In a rare display of tact, however, he refused to disparage his wife to his sons. He harbored no bitterness. In the end, said Adwok's father, it was best to let it all go.

But Adwok's mother did not go, which surprised everyone. Determined to maintain a presence, she appeared like a delayed storm front one day after all tragedies and celebrations, most likely out of respect for the abridged version of their family. She made sure the boys knew her address. Ghostly, she stood at the fringes of school activities, her hair properly covered, her clothes bulky and newly dark.

"It's remorse," Adwok's father said, as she flitted off into a crowd, temporary as a moth.

But to Adwok, who resented her deeply, it was more like she had taken to vacationing frequently in Erkowit or some resort, always coming back rested and slightly heavier, having missed the hard parts of life. The shadows gone from under her eyes.

Though there was talk that she bore the civil servant a child, another son, Adwok's mother never spoke of it to Adwok or David, and Adwok's father did his best to avoid news of her. Adwok saw someone he thought was her once, from a distance, walking near the Mogran, a bright yellow giraffe dangling from one hand and a sloppy-looking child dangling from the other. Trailing a slimy finger through the air, the child skipped a little, or tripped over his feet. Adwok couldn't tell.

That same day he came home to find his father in the yard with a shovel. After all that time, he had gone in to pick up her gravel order. Borrowed a truck, borrowed, even, the shovel.

Adwok thus became aware early on that no paths were straight.

He could never explain his youth to Parissa. She wouldn't have understood. Though she was enamored of the idea of his past, it was clear that she wanted it to be more exciting than it was. Parissa, intent on re-inventing him for maximum entertainment value, snorted when he told her about his middle class neighborhood. She imagined him dirt poor, a child of the streets, maybe a victim of frequent attempts at seduction by low level terrorists.

"My father was a dentist," Adwok said, tapping a slightly yellow incisor with his fingernail.

"Ibrahim Adwok." Parissa cocked a beautifully groomed eyebrow. "You don't have to lie to me. I want to hear all the things other people are too fucking afraid to hear."

He loved her, but she didn't want to understand anything, and really, she didn't have to. Her parents were rich, both of them environmental lawyers living in Santa Barbara. Growing up, she had her pick of private schools. Her father sent her a check every month, huge sums of money camouflaged in envelopes, wrapped in blank sheets of office stationery—*Baqir & Baqir, Attorneys-at-Law*—or old legal papers, never with an accompanying note. Parissa was loud and insouciant, perpetually unhappy. Sometimes she called her parents just to fight with them, her spittle dotting the phone. She insisted she didn't want their money but cashed their checks anyway, complained that her parents were cold towards her, that they never spoke anything but English in the house, but then she'd burst into tears, moaning how desperately she missed them.

For Adwok, trapped on one side of their relationship, it was completely exhausting.

Month after month, Parissa rebelled, even though at twenty-seven she was entirely too old for rebellion. Before him, she had dated a Russian and a Utah Mormon. She listened to Sri Lankan rap, wore electric pink tube tops and dyed snakeskin pants, the tattooed latitudes of jungles crawling up her thighs. Over time, her grammar eroded and she began to affect some ill-imagined street accent. Adwok teased her, told her she was living inside her own private movie. Always, silly as Parissa was, Adwok lived in fear of losing her, of getting dumped for a Persian beefcake bartender languishing in the nightclubs of Camden.

Parissa, half Iranian and half Iraqi, was stunning. In rare moments when she pretended to be unaware of her beauty, she lamented being a "mutt." Most of the time she thought herself clever, called herself a "child of compromise."

She had never left the United States.

When he was a senior in high school, Adwok left the country for the first time and traveled with thirteen students to Greece. He secured his place among them with an application essay entitled "Strategies of Diplomacy in a Shifting World," which placed third in the overall competition even though he had only bullshitted his way through with some drivel about North Korea.

When Adwok told them about his forthcoming adventures among the statues of gods, neither his father nor David were terribly supportive.

"Greece," his father hemmed, his eyes a dull mustard color. "*What* for?" A thyroid condition, entirely self-diagnosed, gave Adwok's father a vague jaundice and brittle fingernails he shed nightly into the carpet, yellow crescents that became embedded between David and Adwok's toes. "Is this something they're making you do?"

"I applied for it, Abby."

Adwok's father shook his head. "Why waste your time? Nothing to see there," he said, waving for some reason in the general direction of the Red Sea. He himself had never even been as far as Aswan.

Later, when they were hanging out in his bedroom, David wondered why anyone in his right mind wouldn't take the money and go to Sweden. "Look," he said, brandishing a magazine, impassive models with stiff hair like dried grass. "Just look. Sweden is the hub for it. Herb. Models."

"It's *educational*," Adwok said. "Don't be an idiot."

"As if a week with Swedish models wouldn't be educational," David said, making a face. "Honestly, you make no sense sometimes."

It didn't matter. Adwok went anyway. Most of the trip was forgettable, shared beds in budget hotels, awkward group dinners in touristy restaurants with names like "Parthenon" and "The Columns." He developed a headache and something akin to snow blindness from studying so much marble, naked hips and shoulders blending into an indistinguishable muscled mass.

In a cold room at the Daphni Monastery in Athens, he saw his first mosaic of Christ Pantokrator, fingers stretched spidery across a Bible, eyes beetled and forbidding. Ruler and judge of all. Filling the apse, the face was bottomless, and Adwok couldn't break away. He stared up at the Pantokrator Christ for hours, long after his classmates had wandered back to the bus for snacks, until finally a guard pinched at his elbow and asked him to leave.

Before he left Athens, he mailed his mother a postcard from the monastery gift shop. Christ Pantokrator, with a note on the back: "I think I want to be this guy when I grow up."

●

A few months after Adwok returned, David won a scholarship to Princeton and left for good. He supplemented his scholarship by working part-time cataloguing microfiche in an almost defunct part of the library, a job he bragged in letters required "next to no effort." Mostly he flipped through magazines. The job afforded him sundries, but nothing close to airfare. Occasionally he'd send something in the mail for Adwok, a t-shirt with a Princeton tiger or an out-of-focus photograph taken by one his girlfriends, a faint, corn-colored eyebrow above a blue eye, a girl's face squished into David's cheek, his hair big and kinky, the New Jersey turnpike blurring by the window. *Greetings from Carnegie Lake,* he wrote on the back of one picture, a new girl draped across his shoulders, his wavy grin seeming to say, "I kind of love America."

When he graduated, neither Adwok nor his father could attend, but afterwards David called to tell them his work visa had come through, and that he was staying in New Jersey.

His father coughed once and handed Adwok the phone.

•

Adwok found himself basically alone and ignored. For a while, he liked it. No vigilant women or knuckles buckling his ear.

His father was there but not there. When he came home from work, he wrapped himself in an old afghan that his wife had made when Adwok was first born, and napped, only waking for a quick meal before going back to sleep. He no longer cared whether Adwok was regular with his prayers or keeping up his grades.

Samir had gone to Stanford on a "legacy" and was waffling between majors in political science and sports journalism, so he could cover the World Cup, naturally. His father paid for his passage back on holidays, and when he had a week or so of free time, he'd meet Adwok for foul beans and *karkadé* on the periphery of the University of Khartoum, where Adwok, halfheartedly, was studying medicine as per his father's wish.

"You should get out, you know," Samir said. "You can't believe how much better it is over there."

Adwok didn't say anything.

"Seriously. The girls, the food. You can walk down the street and do whatever the hell you want."

Adwok wanted to tell him the truth, which was that Samir could do those things because he lived on a cushion of his father's money, and that everyone else had to live in cockroach infested apartments like David and eat freeze-dried food and drive cabs until their eyes dried out. He knew how America worked.

"Have you ever gone to the Getty?" he asked instead.

"That's L.A."

"I know. But you're close enough. Americans drive everywhere, anyway."

"I've been to Candlestick Park a bunch of times," Samir said. "Who knows? You might see me on SportsCenter one day broadcasting live from there."

"Yeah?"

"Yeah," said Samir. "Hey, did you hear about Wiraj? He married some hot girl from Bor. Like a model, you know, but not a model. You believe that?"

"I don't know why he wanted to go get married. Seems stupid."

"What else is he going to do? He didn't go to college. He's just going to do what his father does. Besides, trust me. You'd want to marry this girl if you saw her."

Adwok stood around for another fifteen minutes while Samir talked about how easy it was to get weed if you knew the right people, or if your parents did, and then Adwok swallowed the last of the tea and went home to his quiet house. He tried not to wake his father.

•

Some afternoons, after praying for himself, Adwok prayed for his mother's soul and her successful escape from Omdurman, to, well, somewhere. It was, perhaps, the last time he prayed for anyone's soul. When Parissa had the second abortion, he stopped praying. It felt wasteful somehow, like leaving water running from the tap. Parissa, unlike his mother, lived in a land of choices.

Surely, he thought, for his mother the civil servant was but a way out. Samir, who was obsessed with social standing and whose cousin had married a distant cousin of the Royal Family, confirmed this. But where could she go? Bon Accord, Alberta, maybe, or Dill City, Oklahoma, one of the places in the *World Atlas* she had left behind on the table near the gravel order: Imogen Juna-Adwok—*10 square meters*. There were pink chunks of dried wax between some of the pages, flecks of her bikini line.

•

Though Adwok didn't know it, he would escape, if escaping it can be called, running away from one life into another. It would be another three years until he left, thirty-six months of residency at Soba University Hospital, patients whose faces he couldn't remember and didn't want to. It took that long before Adwok realized he had been fooling himself, that he had never been meant or destined for anything. There was no chance that he had been led astray—there was no astray—but he had been led. He had managed carelessly to take seed in the rough soil at the confluence of the White and Blue Niles. Now he squinted at it, the old idea, through his thin, wiry glasses, the thought of *it*, Dill City, Elk City, something American. Going astray was impossible. *Going* was what mattered.

In a few years, he would be in the United States, in the scab-shaped city of Frederick, Maryland, living a different life, no better or worse than his life in Sudan, merely different, and engineered completely by him, which was what made it worthwhile. He would stare at Parissa, her manic features stilled in sleep to a manageable image on the pillow, and he'd wonder what it would mean for there to be another woman there, or their bed in another city, their pillow made in a different factory. If any of his choices were his.

•

On the day he left, he went directly home from the hospital to the house he had been raised in, the house he had inherited, a dull red Volkswagen parked on the neglected gravel patch. His father was asleep, the sheets pulled up to his chin like a small child.

Adwok had just come for the atlas, but he stayed to tidy up. He left his father the pittance he had earned plumbing the diseased alveoli of people's lungs, and then he left his father. That was okay with him. He strained it, controlled it as he had his temper all those years. He didn't know where he'd go, just somewhere. As he pulled away, he looked back at the flattened gravel pocking the front yard, and then never thought about any of it again.

For the first year, he lived with David on the south side of a duplex in Passaic, New Jersey. Parissa was one of David's roommates from Princeton, though he had of course slept with her. He had slept with everyone. The other roommate was a football player from Texas who packed up after six months but left behind two six packs and a knot of dirty sheets. After he left, Adwok moved his own stuff out of the laundry room and into the football player's, which forever smelled faintly of beer and sweat.

The flights to America had been simultaneously confusing and boring, but Adwok managed successfully to make his way, through accident mostly, getting lost only once in the Frankfurt airport. David didn't do much to explain anything, just picked him up at Newark after an hour through customs and two hours of post 9/11 TSA interrogation.

When he first arrived, she was sitting on the football player's mattress on the floor, rolling an open beer between her ankles. It was before her street period, and she still looked sweet, her inky hair ironed straight, her small fingernails painted a flesh-color. "I'm Parissa." She rocked her head back and motioned for him to join her on the mattress. "Baqir."

He didn't move. "Ibrahim Adwok."

Within an hour, he had learned everything there was to know about her. How her parents had abandoned her to fight the battles of oil-covered fish and nearly extinct birds. She crawled over to the television, the pockets of her cut-off shorts brushing against her thighs. He had never seen a girl's thighs.

"Here, you've got to see this. You're never going to believe how they pimped me out."

She had been a baby model, her face on diapers, a child model at three. One by one, she slid in the videos. Toothpaste and "Mama, I Wet Myself" doll commercials. She said she hated doing them, that her first memories were of being dragged to auditions, her mother smearing her with pancake makeup. She kept playing them, the tapes, over and over again.

"Can you fucking *believe* it?"

He laughed when she wanted him to laugh, was outraged when that was desired, but quietly he wondered if there was something wrong with him, that he wouldn't ever have recognized her as the same creature from the commercials.

Adwok had known before he arrived that he'd have to re-do most of his medical training in the States. Parissa came with him to campus, ate her lunch sitting cross-legged on stone benches while he took remedial chemistry and molecular biology. She was always waiting for him when he came out of class, a piece of paper in her hand with the name of a new place they had to visit or a restaurant one of the students had told her about.

David, who was already with a pre-law girl, Sylvia Berger or Sylvia Bergstrom, didn't say anything when they became lovers, but Adwok knew he wouldn't have minded regardless. As if to prove it, he helped Adwok and Parissa move down to Frederick, the three of them carrying boxes and stepping on rolls of packing tape and each other. After they finished unpacking, they stood around in the tiny backyard drinking beer. Parissa put an arm around both of them.

Samir came for a visit once at a particularly bad time, after they'd been in the house for a couple of years. Parissa had become pregnant for the first time, after uncharacteristically refusing to use birth control, and had terminated the pregnancy three days before, despite Adwok's objections. They had argued for weeks, chasing each other through the house, screaming until the little children that lived on the other side of their fence began to cry, their parents peeking through the slats of wood with only partially disguised looks of disapproval. Everything seemed different then.

Samir arrived driving one of his father's birthday gifts. His hairline had begun to recede, revealing a pale patch of skin, traces of something pathetic and fearful. Unemployed and freshly divorced, he was still all bravado, but he wasn't fooling anybody.

They sat outside on a slab of concrete in the backyard, mosquitoes landing imperceptibly on their fingers. Parissa wouldn't come out. She remained inside with a heating pad, the television on mute.

"What have you heard about Wiraj?" Samir asked. "Do you know if he and that woman from Bor had any kids?"

"I don't hear anything. I haven't really kept in touch with anyone." Adwok wondered how much, if anything, he was obliged to tell his childhood friend. If there was any point in talking about their lives, how it had all worked out. He wished, in a way, they could just go back to playing chess.

"She probably cheated on him. I mean, you saw her, right?"

Adwok shook his head.

"She was Grade A fucking gorgeous." Samir smashed a mosquito between his fingers, leaving a small smear of blood. "And you know, Wiraj. Kind of nothing, that guy. Like a slab of clay. Remember we called him clayface that time?" Samir laughed. "Anyway, she probably left his sorry ass for some guy with money."

Across the fence, the children had come out to play in the dusk. One of them ran, whistling through the grass. They climbed a plastic yellow slide and screamed with delight on their way down.

Samir cleared his throat. "Sorry, man. I hope that didn't sound weird. Your mother and that business."

Adwok blinked, surprised. He hadn't thought of her for some time. Every now and then when he'd notice the atlas. "It's fine."

"Besides," said Samir, "Everyone knows she didn't do it. Everybody knows it was Wiraj's mother screwing around with that guy. She was just covering her ass by saying it was your mother. What a bitch, man. Just proves we didn't know shit back then. Nobody there did."

Adwok realized he had stopped breathing for several minutes.

On the other side of the fence, one child kept saying the other's name, like an incantation. Jacob. Jacob. Jacob.

"But at least we got out, right?"

·

Adwok did get out. His mother wouldn't be so lucky, buried in the hard earth after a stroke at sixty-five, her body wrapped in the proper way.

Wiraj's mother mourned her for forty days, a secret swirl of scotch in her belly as she took her grandchildren to school.

Adwok's father found out about the funeral too late. As a point of pride, he refused to visit her grave, though he locked himself in the bedroom one night and rubbed her afghan against his face until his cheeks were raw. When he finished weeping, he cleared his throat and called David in Passaic to tell him his mother had died, in the most matter of fact tone.

"Tell your brother, won't you?" he asked. As if to soften the blow, he added, "No one expected it."

"Right," said David. "I'll tell him. I'm sorry, I have work."

·

During his residency at Soba, Adwok had taken his lunches with his mother. It wasn't planned; she merely appeared one day at the cafeteria holding a plastic tray with *hilu mur,* a question on her face. He took a bowl of sweet noodles and motioned for her to join him.

Adwok expected her to ask about his studies—he was in the middle of a pulmonary rotation—but she did not. She ate silently across from him, occasionally dabbing at the edge of one cheek. Watching her closely, he noticed things that had escaped him over the years since she had left: four gray whiskers on either side of her mouth and a slight clicking sound of her jaw. Perhaps she had dentures now?

At the end of the meal, she asked him how and where to pay, and he lifted the lanyard with his I.D. card. "They don't mind covering it if you bring a guest now and then," he said.

"I liked your postcard," she said, getting up from the table.

"What postcard?"

"Christ Pantokrator." She must have held onto it for six years. "I had to look that up, Pantokrator."

"Me too," Adwok said.

"World creator."

"Yeah. All fire and brimstone."

She laughed. "What did your father make of it?"

"I don't know," Adwok said. He had only sent it to her.

It wasn't a big deal to him, their lunches. He was working non-stop, barely sleeping at the time. Sometimes they never said anything, just ate and left.

He saw her twice more at the cafeteria. Each time, she had a cold.

She told him about life in Omdurman. She had fallen into some kind of nanny position to the neighborhood children, unpaid of course, and in her spare time she was taking courses at al-Ahfad, the women's college. He tried a couple of times to ask her how she was making money, but she changed the subject.

"How's your foot?" she asked, swallowing her coffee slowly, as if it hurt going down.

"Same as always." He poked it out from under the table, flinging back his lab coat. "Works well enough. Gets me where I need to go."

Adwok's mother smiled. "I always thought it was because you didn't want to leave me." She patted her stomach. "You got all caught up coming out."

"Maybe so," Adwok said. "Or maybe I was pushing off. Couldn't get away fast enough." He had meant for it to be a joke, but it sounded funny coming out, and she looked down at her empty plate.

She didn't look well. When she coughed, it made a low rattle, an echo behind her ribs.

"You know, I can write prescriptions now. I could get you something for that."

She shook her head. "It'll take care of itself," she said.

Adwok smiled awkwardly. He had to get back and she sensed it and got up from the table, collecting her trash.

"Are you sure you don't need any money?" he asked.

She leaned over and kissed him on the cheek, took what was left of her food, and slowly made her way through the plastic tables and chairs, past dozens of young doctors, before reaching up quickly to cover her hair.

MacArthur Park

For reasons they can't fathom, Joanna and Rudy are separated on the plane to Los Angeles by a boy with no legs. They discover him in Joanna's seat when they go to sling their carry-ons into the overhead bin.

The boy looks about fifteen and sits with an *US Weekly* splayed across his crotch, doesn't notice them or refuses to, so deeply involved is he in an article about the ten worst celebrity beach bodies of the summer. His eyes move over a starlet's thighs, her subtle cellulite highlighted by red circles and editorial asides. When the boy reads, he opens his lips, just barely, like a newborn tasting air.

"Excuse me," Joanna says, because someone has to. "I believe this is my seat."

The boy coughs, and one of his thumbs smudges news of someone's failing breast implants. His ears are plugged with either speed metal or the clashing of thirteenth century Turko-Mongol sabers, about which Rudy is something of an expert. From time to time, she imagines giving a lecture near a table covered with gleaming weaponry, her seventh graders in awe, their faces like fresh baked pies.

Trying not to stare, Joanna puzzles over how the boy managed to make his way down the jet bridge to her seat. There hadn't been a wheelchair, at least not that she saw. Her mind moves carefully, as if each thought must be tethered by safety cables to rock. If only they knew what had happened. It shouldn't make a difference, but it does. Too young for the Army, too young for Walter Reed. She doubts it could be congenital; the knees are not smooth and white, no evidence of arrested development. Both women have lived long enough to recognize injury when they see it.

In the 80s, one of Rudy's students lost an eye when he bound five sparklers together. After three months of surgeries, the boy returned to school. Standing in the hall with the other teachers, Rudy watched him bouncing along with his friends as if nothing had happened, the only evidence a black patch over the empty eye socket.

Neither adorned with prostheses nor encased in pant legs, the red curves of what would be the boy's knees remain exposed, tapping to a private beat.

Normally the women wouldn't mind swapping seats with him, but it's a long flight from Atlanta, as well as a special trip—Rudy's retirement after thirty-five years teaching European history and coaching field hockey—and Joanna intends for things to go perfectly, though she's beginning to think that means it will be impossible for her to enjoy herself.

All Joanna wants is to make good memories and cache them away in a trunk under the bed. To have the kind of trip they will feed from when they are too old for travel. The RESPECT concert, five days in the turquoise water of a hotel pool. They can talk about it when they are residents of Rose Hill, the aging, childless couple, both easing into a steady senility that will rob them of their habits of hygiene and courtesy. As long as they have each other and the memory of Los Angeles. Aretha's sequins and the architecture of her hats.

Now Joanna sees them sitting in white metal chairs on an artificial patch of grass, recalling the boy. They won't remember where they had been going, or why, just his absent limbs. It will become a frequent topic of conversation—remember that boy?—along with lost friends, the lobster bisque at The Chowder Pot, and the death of the novel.

Joanna places a hand on the boy's shoulder and applies a quick pressure, enough to make him look up.

"Not sure if you heard me—I believe you're in my seat," she says, halfway apologetically.

Rudy rifles through Joanna's purse for documentation. "Show him your ticket."

"Do what?" the boy says in a monotone.

Joanna smiles. "What I mean to say is, I bought tickets four months ago for my friend and me, together. If you could just scooch over."

The boy returns to his magazine. He makes no movement, save for a slight, impatient vibration. "Not my problem," he says.

After a minute, Rudy shrugs and sits by the window. She yanks out a Ron Chernow presidential biography and buries herself in it, determined to read her way through the flight.

Joanna stares at her. "You're just going to sit."

"I'm tired of standing," Rudy says, not looking up from her book. "So are you."

Joanna, unwilling to concede, waits for a flight attendant, but when one arrives to smash down the bins with her skinny arms, she gestures Joanna down into the other seat. "You need to be buckled for take-off."

The three of them sit silently for the duration of the flight. Only once is there any kind of communication, when the flight attendant comes by with the snack cart. The boy orders a Sprite and doesn't say a word as the drink is handed to him. The sabers clang on in infinite variations of battle in his ears. Rudy and Joanna shake their heads politely and indicate they aren't interested in food or drink, though they are forced to pass a bag of pretzels, and finally, a small napkin, over the boy's missing legs.

*

At LAX the women stride past gift shops and television monitors, through layers of post-flight security, down into tunnels and up escalators, forgetting about the boy. They tip bathroom attendants with the last of their change, and witness tearful reunions at the baggage claim. While waiting, they eat prepackaged sandwiches, fretting while two children climb on the conveyor belt.

They don't take a breath until they collapse in the backseat of a cab. It's then that they notice the sky, a muted blend of pinks and grays tinted with green, a storm waiting far away over the desert. The driver eases out into traffic. He keeps the windows down, one hand wiping sweat off the back of his head. Rudy leans her head against Joanna's shoulder and dozes, fine strands of Joanna's blond hair blowing against her face.

When they finally arrive at the hotel in Westlake, it's well past eleven, but they can instantly see it's not what was advertised, the only accurate detail a pool with a couple of sickly palm trees leaning over it. The women climb out of the cab and navigate their way through shards of glass on the dark asphalt. Near the door, bluish lights illuminate a handwritten warning about large bills and after-hours transactions.

This hotel is in no way responsible for thefts, injuries, break-ins, or alterca-tions with other guests. Please enjoy your stay! —The Management

Inside the lobby, someone has at least made the effort to create the illusion of luxury—leather furniture, a plasma television, a faux marble desk. But the twin ferns are dead, and cigarette butts and dead flies are in piles in the corners of the floor. The television is showing an entertain-ment program on a loop. Lindsay, Sandra, Paris, Katie, Lindsay.

Joanna and Rudy are too tired to protest.

At the desk, a taciturn clerk takes Joanna's credit card and proffers keys by smacking them down on the counter like playing cards. Joanna is charged at least twenty dollars more than she was quoted, via mysteri-ous fees and hotel surcharges, but she is so eager for sleep that she lets it go. Rudy inquires how far it is to the nearest non-chain restaurant, and the woman hands her another card, this one the number for a $40 per trip private driver.

"We can't walk to anything from here?" Rudy asks.

The woman waves long, leopard-colored fingernails. "It's MacArthur Park." She makes a face like Rudy has suggested jumping off the Capi-tol Records building, but a second later, her eyes go soft. "I guess, if you want."

There is no one to take their stuff or walk the women to their room, so they haul their bags through the mildewed stucco corridor, past an unconvincing mural of a vineyard, and up a narrow flight of stairs. The elevator, of course, is out-of-order.

The room reeks of cigarettes, and when Rudy collapses on the bed and pulls back the sheets, she finds more than a couple questionable hairs coiled on their pillows.

"I'm going to take a shower," Joanna sighs, rifling through her bags. She plunges her hands down into layers of folded clothes, searching for pajamas. It took her five days to pack, unpacking, re-packing, shifting things around. Really, she needed so little. A dress or two for dinners out and the Aretha concert, some stylish walking shoes and a new bathing suit. Yet each time she walked through a room, she found herself grab-bing something she could vaguely imagine using. After a while, it no longer felt like she had to decide what to bring but what to leave behind.

Rudy, meanwhile, packed the night before, rolling everything into a tight ball. Two outfits, a toothbrush, and a bar of soap.

"Seriously. It's not safe to walk to anything?"

Joanna stares through the heavy yellow curtains at the blaze of traffic lights and fast food signs. "Maybe we should've rented a car."

"I don't buy it. How much you wanna bet they get a kickback from the driving service."

"It's not too late to find a different hotel. We can probably get our money back."

In the dim light, Rudy appears younger, less gray in her hair. The first night they slept together, Joanna told her she looked like a younger Gladys Knight. Rudy laughed so hard she fell off the bed.

"Let's talk about it in the morning. You relax and take your shower."

"Hey Ru," Joanna says, disappearing into the bathroom. "I think we should find out where Aretha's staying."

·

Despite the room's shortcomings, the hot water stays good for nearly an hour, and Joanna reclines in the tub, letting it blast until her skin puckers. Sticking out of the shower curtain is a little tag that reads: "Made in Thailand," though someone has crossed out the Thai and written "LaLa" land.

Joanna can still salvage this trip. She closes her eyes and breathes in the steam. A massage, maybe. The pipes groan on the other side of the wall as someone turns on the faucet, and the water pressure is immediately halved. She grabs a bar of soap and runs a hand over her chest, across the wormy scar. It reminds her, always, of a worm in an apple.

"The Wound" was what Rudy called it when they first met, both of them reluctant inductees into St. Joseph's Breast Cancer Survivors Group. Every Thursday, fourteen pale women in shapeless sweatshirts met in a room to talk about "what they would reclaim," according to the uplifting brochure. Participation in the group was allegedly an essential part of their recovery. They even had homework.

Rudy, having endured a double mastectomy, had no patience for the stuffed animals and pink ribbons, the life affirmations and the love letters to themselves. She sat in the back of the room making wisecracks under her breath and knotting little pink nooses for her teddy bear.

At first, Joanna didn't know what to make of her. A fiftysomething school teacher from New Mexico with an interest in siege weapons and a propensity for mom jeans. Rudy was not necessarily someone she could imagine seeing a movie with. All of Joanna's friends were in their thirties, mostly white, wealthy lawyers from her firm with overachieving spouses and polyglot kids.

Joanna felt weak and uncomfortable around strangers, and she found herself enjoying Rudy's easy company. Together they sat in the back by posters of reproductive organs and partially developed embryos, eating M&Ms and snickering.

If Rudy was unsure of Joanna, she didn't show it. The day Joanna showed up with a teal silk scarf around her head, Rudy laughed and told her she didn't need it, that she shouldn't buy into "all the scarf-and-padded-bra crapola." She went to Joanna's house when Joanna was still in the thick of alternating rounds of radiation and chemo, and wrapped a blanket around her on the couch. Joanna was so nauseous she couldn't keep anything down, but Rudy did her best to distract her, showing her shiny photographs of bronze sabers from the Met catalog.

When they celebrated the end of Joanna's treatment by going to a bar and ill advisedly chasing their meds with whiskey sours, Joanna thought she had found a new best friend. Drunk and careless, she admitted to Rudy that she was ashamed to still have both her breasts. That she hated herself for ending a five year relationship because everything her girl-friend thought about seemed trivial. Guilty that she was young enough at thirty-five to have children, if she wanted.

Rudy laughed. She reached across the bar and grabbed Joanna's face. "Hell yeah," she said, and kissed her.

•

Joanna climbs into bed and presses herself into Rudy's back, her chin stamping a crescent of moisture on her neck. Rudy pushes back against her for warmth. They keep the air conditioner cranked up to drown out two men fighting outside.

"An inauspicious beginning," Joanna mumbles into her shoulder blade.

"I tried leaving the television on," Rudy says. "I thought maybe we could fall asleep with it, like white noise. It's stuck on Telemundo. Not Telemundo, some kind of Spanish porn thing. A guy with a bad handle-bar mustache is giving it to a girl in a beer wench costume. I got through maybe ten minutes, but he has a plastic scabbard."

Joanna laughs. "I don't wanna think what's under these sheets. Oh Jesus. *Bedbugs.*"

"Don't even."

They hold each other for a while, feeling phantom insects on their legs. Ten minutes, twenty, and Rudy begins to snore. It will start softly, as if she has food in her mouth. By midnight it will be a click, punctuated sometimes by a moan. By morning, a dry rattle. Ever since the chemo,

Joanna sleeps for no more than three hours, and even then it's shallow. She nurses her worry through the hours, comforted somehow by Rudy's oblivion, the sound of her tongue settling against the roof of her mouth. It helps Joanna measure out what's left of the dark.

After some time, she thinks about the boy from the plane. Perhaps he's somewhere in downtown Los Angeles, rolling under the yellow lights. They never even learned his name.

When the plane landed, Joanna got up first to let him out. She watched as he reached under the seat and retrieved a backpack, unzipped it, and pulled out a skateboard. Effortlessly he lowered himself to the floor, took two steps on his knuckles, lifted his torso onto the skateboard, and was off.

Joanna followed him down the aisle, her knees nearly brushing the back of his head as they waited for people to retrieve their bags. She felt foolish, imagining he would have needed their help. At some point, the boy pulled out a cell phone and started talking. "Nope," he said. "It's tomorrow." He made his way past the stewardesses who smiled down at him, and up the ramp, scraping along with his fists. "Yeah man. I'm here. Easy fuckin' peasy."

At five in the morning, Joanna opens her eyes. Rudy's awake, her legs dangling over the edge of the bed. The brakes of a garbage truck groan a few blocks away.

"Is it those guys from last night?" Joanna asks.

Rudy turns, deep hollows of sleeplessness pitting her face. "I just woke up for some reason and couldn't go back to sleep." She pulls the bedspread around her shoulders, fingering the pattern of cigarette burns. "You're the damn insomniac."

"All day on the plane couldn't have helped."

"I'm fine. Just cold and wide awake."

Eventually she climbs back in next to Joanna, and they both watch the light edging through. "I think we should take a walk in MacArthur Park tomorrow. Broad daylight."

"Ru. Don't joke."

"Just around the lake. I can't tell my kids we were right across from it and we didn't even see it."

Joanna kisses her forehead and rolls away from her.

Later that morning while Rudy is sleeping, Joanna drinks coffee and eats cornflakes downstairs, the news on low. The lobby is nearly empty, save for the same desk clerk working the last hours of her night shift. Leaning against the desk, a man with a mustache and an expensive suit speaks to her in half whispered Spanish. After Joanna looks over at him one too many times, the man raises his eyebrows at her.

"You need to go somewhere?" He brandishes the same card they received the night before. *Fleet Driving Service, LLC.* "Ripley's, Grauman's. Wherever you're going."

She shakes her head and looks away, turning her attention to the television. A liquor store robbery and an elderly woman found dead in a car. *Now for some good news,* the anchorman says. *Last week we told you about a dog in Echo Park that had been severely beaten and burned by his owner. Well, we're happy to report that Hex has now found a home.* A photo appears on the screen, a small, furless dog with stitches holding his flanks together.

"Wonderful," Joanna says. "I'd kill myself if I lived here."

Rudy walks in and grabs a handful of powdered donuts, the fire from an Oakland explosion burning on the screen.

"You should try and catch a nap," Joanna says.

"I'm thinking of becoming a vampire," she says, her lips caked with sugar. "The glittery kind, but black."

"Too bad you're retired. Your students would love it."

"Oh yeah." Rudy gobbles another donut and glances out the window at the sickly palms and splayed pool chairs. "So. Feel like floating?"

"If you want something healthier, they have bananas over there. And yogurt."

"Jo-Jo."

"Okay, fine." Joanna sets down her coffee. "Let's float."

Rudy does her best impression of a seventh grader on a snow day. *"I'll float. You just try not to sink."*

With the exception of a teenage girl in a blue bikini, they have the pool to themselves. Joanna treads water at the far end and stares at her legs. In the refracted light, they appear longer, as if she's a circus performer on stilts. Rudy floats in the shallows, water collecting in the empty foam bra of her bathing suit. She flexes her feet, spraying microscopic beads of water Joanna's way.

"Come get a load of me, Jo."

Joanna wades over and places her palms flat under Rudy's spine, even though she doesn't have to. Rudy's body is made for floating, with her fleshy hips and paddle thighs.

No matter how many times Joanna tries, her body proves incapable of floating, something that Rudy finds hilarious. "Everybody can float," she insists.

Joanna prefers laps, sidestrokes and butterflies that take her from one end of the pool to the middle in a single push.

In Vegas, on their first anniversary, the women swam in a stone pool stocked with fish, wedged between two artificial waterfalls. "It's saltwater," Rudy said. "Foolproof." Joanna floated for three seconds before her head went under and she came face to face with the open mouth of a dartfish.

Rudy weighs nothing, and Joanna slowly spins her, watches her stare up at the clouds.

"I wish I could wear a little bikini like that girl."

"She's a teenager, Ru."

Rudy cranes her head to look at Joanna, her face elfin with strands of hair plastered over her ears. "I know. But it'd be nice to be able to fill it out."

Small black beetles float near Joanna's shoulders, and Rudy threads her fingers through the water and moves them off.

They stay in the pool for two hours, until their skin is wrinkled and numb. When they can't take the cold any longer, they swim up to the far side and stare out past the palm trees at MacArthur Park. Late afternoon, and they spot a man walking a pit mix. A cluster of women sitting on blankets, blasting a stereo.

"It doesn't look bad at all," Rudy says, pulling herself out.

*

That evening the women sit in the lobby, thigh-to-thigh on a brown leather loveseat, waiting to be retrieved by the driver.

Joanna has squeezed herself into a dark red dress, has flat-ironed her hair into yellow sheets that fall over her shoulders. Rudy wears her birthday present to herself, a green silk caftan. Both women are wearing earrings for the first time in months, and Joanna finds her piercings have nearly closed up in the interim.

When the driver finally arrives, fifteen minutes late, the women jump to their feet and hurry to the door.

"Have a nice time," the clerk says, her palms flat on the faux marble.

They don't say anything on the drive over, but their stomachs gurgle. It's been years since they've seen a live concert. Not since Tori Amos gyrating on a piano bench, back when they were new lovers. In the car, they hold hands, their knuckles against the warm leather. A couple of blocks from the Staples Center, the driver drops them off and tells them to call when they're ready to return to the hotel.

The next three hours, Joanna and Rudy are on their feet in a sea of people, everybody dancing and singing, glowing bracelets sliding on their arms. When Aretha takes the stage, Rudy cheers so loud her voice breaks. Joanna isn't much on live concerts—being sandwiched in a sweaty crowd—but she finds herself getting into it. When Rudy sings along with "I Never Loved a Man," Joanna smiles at her like they are privy to the last real secret in the world.

After the concert, they rush out into the street. Glancing into window after window, they end up in a fancy wine bar where everyone has drinks and sits on padded stools, holding the impossibly thin stems of expensive wine glasses. They look around for a menu or a waiter but can find neither, so they fill their empty stomachs with Pinot Noir. Rudy keeps her hand on Joanna's knee all night, her eyes following the path of wine down Joanna's throat, deeper into a warm spot somewhere inside her chest, and eventually back up like a wave to her face.

"Aretha!" Joanna shouts. She hears herself not sounding like herself. Like a bird. A hawk. "I fucking love that woman!"

"Language!" Rudy filches some sushi samples from a passing waiter who ignores her.

Joanna has never felt happier. She had hoped for this, to sit across from Rudy and not feel tired. To mark their lives in an unforgettable way. Now, maybe for the first time, she likes the uncertainty, the fact that she can't predict the future. Persuaded by the chemicals in her bloodstream, the muscles in her shoulders unwind, and she swings her legs from the stool. Her shoes pop off her heels and dangle from her toes.

In the orange glow of the bar, Rudy's cheeks look like green apples. She keeps offering Joanna tiny squares of tuna and shark, trying to fill her stomach, but Joanna turns her mouth away like a child. "You need to eat something," Rudy says. Joanna lifts the shark to Rudy's mouth instead and forces it between her lips.

A constant din rises around them, silverware and laughter, the purring of waiters, but for once Joanna isn't worried or distracted. She isn't thinking about where she has to be tomorrow morning, or about Rudy's next follow-up with the oncologist, or about the pros and cons of redoing the upstairs bathroom. The hum of people around her bolsters her, elevates her, pulls her closer. She drinks another glass of the Pinot, and then finishes Rudy's glass for her.

After a while, there are no more sharp edges.

●

Joanna is in the bar bathroom straightening herself up when Rudy makes the call. She sits at a glass vanity, trying to bring her face into focus. Unable to make out the subtle details of her eyes, only the line of her mouth and the shape of her hair, Joanna is vaguely aware that the cleavage of her dress has migrated lower than it should be. She tugs it back up to hide the scar. Though she can't make it out in the swath of red fabric, she knows where it is, dead against her skin.

A white lotus floats in a glass bowl near the door, and on the way out, Joanna grabs the petals and rubs them between her fingers. She knows she's close to the edge of what she'll remember tomorrow, that important things will go missing by morning. She makes a deal with herself to remember the taste of the wine, of Rudy's mouth. The music throbbing in her brain.

Rudy's arm is supporting her when they walk out into the street. She's too drunk to notice that the vehicle she's tumbling into, her dress up around her hips, isn't the private car but simply a cab. Her head feels heavy and warm, and she rests her cheek against the cool window.

The drive along Figueroa is bumpy, fast enough for the women to slide into each other across the slick seat. The cab smells vaguely of pickles, or of something that's been pickled, a sharp odor that Joanna wakes to each time she dozes off. She tries to decipher the string of letters in the driver's name but sees an alphabet of consonants. Outside the window people wait at stop lights, under the awnings of stores, young men who wax and wane.

Joanna squints at a woman crossing the street towards a cigar shop, a toddler holding her hand. She thinks it's a toddler, but it doesn't move like a toddler.

"What the hell kind of pet is that?"

"Close your eyes, Jo-Jo," Rudy says.

Joanna is aware, if only liminally, that Rudy is in control and how unusual this is. If she is honest with herself, she will admit that despite the fact that Rudy has been in charge of thousands of seventh graders over the course of thirty-five years, she still sees Rudy, in all significant ways, as incapable. She can't understand why this is, just *that* it is, a knowing that has seeped into her body in the seven years they have been together.

Maybe it's because Rudy only stumbled into Joanna by accident, her first woman after a lifetime married to a man in New Mexico, as mother to a nearly grown daughter and son, all of whom abandoned her after she told them the truth. She made a bed with her fake family. Let them make something with her, out of her, for decades, before she realized. Joanna has always felt sorry for Rudy, but for all the wrong reasons. Not because she lived a lie for so long, but because she was too blind, too incapable, to know it was a lie.

•

When Joanna comes around, she realizes she's outside. The air feels different. Awake with her head on the green silk of Rudy's lap, the protuberance of Rudy's chin above her, the hard, cold resistance of a concrete bench under her. Downtown L.A. fills the edges of the sky where there should be stars.

Rudy looks out ahead.

Though Joanna is not yet herself, her mouth bone dry, one of her shoes gone, she knows where they are.

"I will never forgive you for this," she says. Even drunk, she is aware that there is much she will never forgive Rudy for. That she can't know how far she will go to withhold forgiveness.

Rudy stares ahead at the bands of people. So many, just in this one place, on this one night. Some move quickly on the sidewalks, clutching bottles wrapped in paper bags against their thighs. Others wander the patches of grass, circle, and collapse in a heap, crackling like dead leaves. They wear black and white, patchy blankets over their shoulders, or loose jeans and tight wifebeaters, ball caps and skull caps. No one looks particularly menacing. An old, broken man or woman with hair like a prophet, hands fluttering, head rocking, walks along as if he cannot stop.

"I know," Rudy says.

Joanna should walk away. The hotel is just across the street, blue lights visible. She will have to leave Rudy, walk by the men on the ground, cigarettes dangling from their lips. Wait for the cars to pass. She listens to sirens from some worse off part of town. "I'm leaving," she says, but she doesn't move.

Pennies shine at the bottom of the lake.

●

Joanna remembers when she was eighteen, straight out of high school. She postponed college for a year and went to live near a food co-op run by her uncle and a bunch of hippies in Northern California. Every season but winter they grew and harvested something—cranberries, apples, sunflowers, yams—and every season but winter they slept outside in a barn. They woke to different people, strangers, whom they offered fruit.

Joanna walked into town once a week and called her mother from a payphone to lie to her. "Yes, we just had roast beef. Aunt Susan's roast beef. No, no drugs. Uncle Jim wouldn't hear of it."

That summer, Joanna lost her virginity. Tamara Danelle Henley. In the woods where Uncle Jim grew and harvested cranberries in the ponds, they stripped, their hair floating, tangled in berry stems. Afterward, they licked pond water from each other's fingers. In the afternoon they went back to the group, their skin smelling like peat moss. The girls stayed apart from each other for the rest of the day, as if being close might give them away.

The last time Joanna saw her Uncle Jim, he was smoking weed near the bonfire, in his bathing suit. He waved as her mother yanked her by the hair into the Buick.

●

Joanna presses her foot into the dirt, forcing it to yield. She wishes that something big would happen, something to make this moment seem less important, less memorable. That her dead mother would appear scolding, yanking her away, Joanna's long hair in her fist. An angry animal on the loose, its parts poorly stitched together. A leg by the lake, a tail by the bandshell. An earthquake to open the ground, send them clawing their way out.

Joanna finds Rudy's fingertips under the stone bench.

A cop has begun to patrol the periphery, shining a search light back and forth. The light dances across them and stops before moving on, as if it doesn't know yet what it wants to find.

The Yana Land

Maxwell Yana whispered a story in my head, his lips so close my ear begin to thaw.

Listen here, he said, the words rattling behind his mossy teeth. I tried to swat him away, but he advanced slow and deliberate. Once upon a time, he had been like a yellow dog, eager and jumping. Now this was Yana, draggin' himself in the skin of something, in what's left of it.

We were burnin' the last of the *Faith,* everything but the copper hull, a few stray timbers from the stern to feed a pitiful flame. Couldn't get no real fire from it. I thrust my dead fingertips into that orange heat, watched it dance and lick at the green flesh.

Leave off, Yana, I said. Leave me some peace. Can't ye see I'm tryin' to get warm?

There was no warm. I don' remember warm now, anymore. Like some thing you had as a child, you could never have again.

I've found it, he slobbered, pointing a trembling finger. *Aye, the land of wild horses and fresh rivers, with enough grass to fill our bellies for weeks! Trees so far as the eye can see, an' you know what that means, don' ye? Meat! Fire!*

Leave off me, won't ye? I shoved him, I did. His chest sunk so as I coulda put a hole in with my fist. His breath, stinking of bird skin, hung as a mist beclouding us both.

We got fire, Yana, fool! I saved the last of the top-mast, see.

Nah. 'Twont last. An' then what? He chewed at his fingertips, a habit all the men had taken to with a fierceness.

Whaddye care, idiot. You'll be spookin' them birds with your trap.

Ain't no more birds, Cap'n, he said. It was the first truth he told.

For a month or so last December, Yana and Haines stood lookout for them snow geese. They'd nestle themselves in the ground like rats, wait for 'em to get tired and land somewhere, puffing out their feathers with a sigh. Then the men'd pounce. A snow goose may fill two stomachs, more if you stretch 'em out. But Yana was right, and they never came no more, like forgetful grandchildren. Now, we just watched the sky for their feathers, falling in them graceful circles.

Why don't you go and look fer some, then?

You ain't heard me out. He dragged his blackened leg behind him, almost in the fire. He didn't feel nothing. *I've something to tell.*

It was the third story that day, an' I thought I'd slap his slab skull. Were it not I felt sorry for him, nothing to do but jabber to keep his mouth from freezing. He had tried his stories on James and Banks, an' they walked out on the floes to escape him.

But you 'ave to hear it, he said, easing up to me like a baby seal, all slick with grease. *You simply must.*

His hair was fallin' out in patches, like a cat with mange, and he walked in that teeter-totter way all the men did now, listing starboard. There were feathers stuck to his lips.

So tell it then, I said. Tell them all. An' if I fall asleep dead while you tell it, don't make a spectacle of it, just close my eyes, and shove me across, over there, where the water is blackish and deep.

Yana the numbskull, disposing of my remains. Ah, what would Nell say if she saw her sweetheart skittered across the ice by a simpleton? I'd hate to feel her heart, all chopped up. Probably searching the face of the mailman for news, small hands playing across her mouth. At night, she'd be worryin' and twistin' the hem of her sleepclothes like she was trying to restore blood to some lost limb.

My words are no good to her out here, sitting at the bottom of me. When one of them glaucous gulls blows by, I'd like to try an' catch it, have it fly on back to Nell. No use putting letters in a bottle. Bottle'll sink eight feet and freeze, suspended forever. Pains me to think of 'em letters, drawings too, all salty and blurred.

Cap'n, I think you'll be liking this story, Yana said. *It'll give you something to tell them folks when we return.*

Don't be tellin' jokes, I said. I ain't in the mood for no jokes.

What jokes, sir? Yana rubbed his stomach all round n' round like.

That bird skin don't digest too kindly. I warned 'em all against the Greenland parrots, but they ate what they could find. They have such high hopes, these fools, like this place can't crush out. They're waiting for them snow geese like Santa Claus.

You know what jokes. Telling about *return.* Like the other day, when you says you seen a schooner? Got everyone all excited, running to the edge of them floes? M'Clure almost killed ye. Aye, the fire's dyin' out. Christ.

No jokes, sir. Not in my story. Why, don't ye want to hear? I'm talking 'bout, I found new land! Over there, where you see that ice.

'Tis no land, imbecile. 'Tis a mirage. They call 'em fata morgana.

But I found it! I did! 'Tis the Yana Land, sir.

Ah, stop yer jawboning. I swear ye, that is an ice island.

Yana was so excitable, the blood ran out his nose mercilessly. Clean yourself up, won't ye? I said. Yer a sight.

My head was splitting. The ice contracted, eatin' at the *Faith's* copper hull. Digging in. When the timbers broke, it made a terrible noise, like something tearing the world apart, and the men went out to get away from it. They kicked a ball around, or shot at bears in the distance. I had no such luxury, for a captain remains with his vessel. I stayed, and it felt like the ice was closing in on my skull.

Fire's dyin.'

It's something to draw on them maps. So as we didn't come out here for nothing. So as—

My fist slammed him down on its own. I swear to you, I didn't have the strength. Out it went, steady as a gun brig. When you hit a man who's half dead already, there's nothing at all to it. His mouth was mush, teeth loose from scurvy, gums bleedin' from before. There weren't no sound when he hit the ice.

Git up and tell it, then, I said. Tell like a real storyteller.

His face was turned away at an awkward angle, such as like he was looking for one of 'em sea pigeons.

When I realized he was dead, I nudged him with what was left of my boot. I shoved him real slow over to the pile at the edge of the floe. I didn't say nothing—nobody said much anymore nowadays, except for Yana and his damn stories—but I looked up where the deck used to be, where there used to be a watchman, and I realized no one had seen.

None of us watched each other. They were free men, once the *Faith* was gone.

Yana, I thought. Ye are a lucky man. 'Tis over. But I admit a secret shame I never heard his story. Twas probably a better story than what has happened to us.

*

It's been two years since the ice stopped us, but I don't count no more. I go by absences. No more cheese. No beer, nor bread. The lemon juice ran out back when that white terrier of Finlay's disappeared with the wolves, weeks and weeks ago. I tried to grow some mustard in the hull, but it won't take. In February, the salt beef was gone. In April, the first year, the dried peas. Them days weren't all that bad.

In t'beginning, we thought we had a chance. Patience. Wait out the winter, and the ice would shift. It did sometimes, bringing her up, taking her back down. Always wedged but good. We spent days chopping our way out, only to have our work undone the next morning, like 'en by some cursed ice fairy. The second summer, the ice lifted the *Faith* out of the water five feet, and then swung forty degrees to port. All our hopes were up. We were runnin' around a lot in them days, smashing into each other. Seemed like everything was so important, like every minute something was happenin'. I told the men to wear all their clothes, case 'en we had to leave the boat in the night, should the ice break it up. They've had on their clothes now for two years, what's left of 'em.

In this place, there is no such thing as time. You kill a walrus in the spring, eat what you can, and the rest will sit out there forever. I'm bettin' the whale that dies on the floor of this ocean is the whale that never goes nowhere.

The first night when it happened, the men were running with their axes, and I was shoutin' orders. It got real quiet on deck, and I could hear everything. I was staring out, looking for the cracks, and I saw this chunk of ice, but it weren't no ice. Polar bear, just the head poking up, staring right at me. Them eyes, I'll never forget. Then he was gone.

Animals that used to come around got smart, got outta here. White whales. Unicorns, with them tusks poking out like corkscrews. We used to watch from the deck as they popped up through some small hole in the ice to breathe. They were so stupid they'd get themselves stuck, the hole smaller and smaller, smaller and smaller. We never could get to 'em when they drowned. Floated off somewhere, under the ice.

But we don't see nothing now they've smartened up. Just Jimmy.

Haines raised him by hand, from a skinny, mottled brown kit. Only animal left on this floe. Ye wouldn't know our straits, if ye saw that fox, scampering, biting off chunks of clothes, rotten flesh, carrying pieces of an old air balloon. He thinks it's all a game. He's lucky to have made it so long with such fuzz in his head. Finlay ain't at all sentimental. He'll club him soon as he catches 'im.

Aye, the men are free men, to kill and be killed. A long time ago, they finished being themselves. Maybe when the vessel was gone. The last of the timbers. Back when they ate the dogs and the candles, and then the clothes. They walk away on the ice, and they could go anywhere, but they end up nowhere.

Fire's down to sparks. Last of the great ship, *Faith of My Fathers.*

In t'beginning, I gave 'em all hard jobs. They took axes to the condensation, where it'd build up from their cooking. Kept 'em filling the *Faith's* cracks with oakum. Put 'em in the harness and had them pull the sleds out for miles, pretendin' there was some way out. Jump jacks. Gave 'em a wolf pup to play with.

I wish I had given something to Nell. Some baby, would grow up to be a strong man. Maybe come out one day to find me, bury me for her. Bury her one day. But she'll forget about me. It won't take long. Things happen faster there. Here nothing breaks down.

It took a long time for the *Faith* to die, months on months. 'Twas not like I imagined it, from paintings and books, a great splitting of timbers, men screaming and tossed about. Nah, 'twere slow, an' we just one night walked away when there was nothing more to hope for. We just lifted our legs, calm as cranes, and abandoned her. From then on, we weren't men anymore. Just animals.

Yana started to tell his stories. Fattest woman in the world, what she has for dinner. Smallest man's shoe size. Not stories, really. He didn't know how to tell a story proper. He just liked to tell what he could, so as to feel he had something, some power. *I've got one for ye!* He'd shout, limpin'. Even when he fell out on the ice and got frostbite, we had to cut him, and he turned that into a story too. *One of 'em elephants got me,* was what he'd say. *Stomped me leg, see.*

I remember one day, not so long after we got stuck, I was out walking alone on the ice, and I must've had some kind of look on my face, 'cause Yana comes running out and says he wants to show me something. I thought it was another one of his stories, see. So I follow him, and he shows me this bear, a brown one, not more than fifty yards away. I got

James to bring the gun, and we all just lay there, bellies to the floe, with the gun on him. Must've been hours. He just didn't move, I tell ye. *Maybe he's dead, sir,* is what Yana says. But then I look up, squint me eyes all funny like, and I realize it's a goddamn mouse, just a few yards away. It's all frozen, waiting to see what we're goin' to do. It could've waited for days like that, wonderin' if we were gonna eat it. James jumped up and tried to grab it, but it was gone like that, tunneling off somewhere.

'Tis how it is here. Can't trust nothing you see. I keep walking over to kick at Yana, see if maybe that's an illusion too.

Aye, Yana weren't so bad. A few months ago, I got real sick. It didn't matter to the men. They were drunk, burning off the foremast, spitting flames and blood. Thought it might be the end of me. I propped myself up against what was left of the forecastle, and closed my eyes. Tried to think of Nell, her face and feet. There was this low thumpin' sound, kind of spooky-like—them belukhas bumpin' their heads up against the ice to get air. I fell asleep listening to that sound. Then all of a sudden, that Yana is on top of me, dripping something on my lips. Blood from his sock.

Drink it, sir, will ye? 'Taint your time.

It's all our time, I says. I licked my lips. The blood was warm.

How else we gonna get home? Yana asked.

About broke my heart, poor fool. Yana had them stories.

They say the Eskimo have stories, but I don't believe 'em. I saw them some time the first spring, and they had nothing to say. Five men Eskimos. Drifting off the floes in one of them skin boats of theirs, dressed in rags. Aye, would you look at that? I said to the men. They ain't even shipwrecked and they look as bad off as us.

A few of the men went over to them, waving their arms. The Eskimos just stared, still as stones. James took off his shirt and waved it around.

Yana, oh he was always simple. Always had them stories that go nowhere, just fall down out of his mouth onto the snow. Don't even melt the snow. Yana kept shoutin' at 'em Eskimos, telling about his fat lady and the elephant that stomped his leg. Rainbows. He was all excited about rainbows. Triple one had arched over the boat a day before. So Yana, he just ran up and down, telling and telling.

Them Eskimos, they had nothing to say. They knew we weren't going nowhere. They just sat there in their rags, licking their red lips, chewin' their raw meat. They had them marble eyes, all shiny, and they watched. Just watched.

Everything Gets Mixed Together
at the Pueblo

Everybody is supposed to be on the bus at 12:15.

This is everybody, most of them white. There are a lot of them, small and tall, fat and pale, but if you are looking down at them from the pueblo, they just look like golf tees lined up, brittle and wooden.

Kind of like this: I II I II II III I I

The bus will take everybody up to the pueblo to see the Indians, who are already there now, holding sweaty McDonald's drinks in their hands, staring out from behind screen doors. Waiting for everybody to come up.

Everybody meets outside the Visitor Center, by the stone wall, with access to some enterprising Indian vendors who have walked down from the pueblo to sell bowls, key chains, and miniature terra cotta animals. The vendors wear sunglasses and tee-shirts with basketball team names on them, and sometimes caps turned to the side. They sit at their tables, not talking. They pant a little, as if being around everybody is like being out too long in the sun.

Everybody touches the pots and the terra cotta animals, murmuring admiration. Some of them won't buy anything at the asking price for fear of being deceived, duped by the cunning Indians. Every dollar subtracted from the price is a small victory for them, like planting tiny flags in the fat of their hearts.

A voice announces the imminent bus departure over an intercom. "Please be ready," it asks, without sounding like it is asking.

Everybody has to go to the bathroom before they board the bus. They take their children, whose cheeks are pink and whose mouths twist down into fussy sneers, into the stalls, where sounds of protest echo against the sandstone. The children are then taken by their hands to the sink, where water runs down artfully into a slit from a New Age faucet.

"*No!* Don't *want* to wash our hands," the children say.

"The bus is leaving, come on," the pink parents snap.

Outside, there are brown Indian children, or "Native Americans," as the pink people call them. They run in the heat and laugh. They do not sweat. They do not wash their hands, nor are they made to wash their hands. They urinate in the outhouses on their own and without coercion, or they squat and defecate in the street, where their feces will later be eaten by dogs.

The Pueblo parents love their children, but they allow them run to the end of the cliffs, and they neither worry about nor keep track of their bowel movements. Occasionally, as a result, the children fall to their deaths, or their stomachs explode before they can be taken down to a doctor. Most of the time, though, they are happy, living with disparate things, long shorts and tennis shoes, poverty and worms that burrow into the soles of their feet. In a way, they resemble the pink children, but only superficially, with their buzzcuts and tee-shirts that read "Patriots" and "Dontcha Wish Your Girl Was Hot Like Me."

The brown children run to the edge of the mesa and look down at the pink children below, about to be taken up by the bus. They laugh and throw rocks down. Their parents do not say a word.

*

It's 12:15. Everybody gets on the bus.

They file in and plop down in their seats, ignoring the Indian driver and the Indian guide, both women in long shorts and sandals, with straight black hair that streams over their rounded shoulders. The guide's name is Jennifer. The driver, Kathy.

"Everybody please sit down. This bus will take you to the top of the pueblo," Jennifer says, her voice flat and trained.

"Here we go," the parents say, putting their arms around their children. "Are you ready to see some real live Native Americans?"

As the bus pulls away, the adults turn and watch the Visitor Center disappear in the dust behind them.

Everybody is shocked when they first see the Visitor Center, a massive structure constructed of the finest pale pink sandstone, according to the most refined architectural principles, with special museum wings jutting off to the side like spider legs. Some are unable to fathom that the building represents the Indians they think they know, the ones with drinking problems who live in the gutted hulls of dead cars. There is a fountain spouting precious water in a never-ending vomitous flow from the mouth of a bird. No wooden cigar store Indian chiefs. Music is piped outside, something with flutes and chanting. Everybody enters cautiously, meeting with the brightness of marble and the exhilaration of air conditioning.

On the bus, everybody misses the air conditioning.

"Could you please open another window? It's pretty hot back here," a middle-aged white woman immediately asks. They have only been on the bus for sixteen seconds, but they have already determined their maximum level of discomfort. They are not afraid to speak out when they want something, and what they want is comfort and air conditioning and possibly some pretzels. But they should not be judged for this, for the Indians have a level of comfort as well, even if their bodies function like sand or water or stone, taking millennia to adjust.

Jennifer and Kathy ignore the passengers.

Some of the more sensitive people do their best to win them over. There is admiration for the female Native Americans, with their grave faces and horse-tail thick hair, but everybody is afraid to show too much of this admiration for fear of patronizing them.

"What a lovely visitor center that was," a sensitive man finally says on the bus, patronizing the Indians, because he cannot help it, because it has welled up inside him and he truly was impressed by the tremendous wood door that opens like a secret passage on an immensely expensive hydraulic system.

"Thank you," Kathy answers, in a low tone, not because she has to, but because, in a way, she *is* proud of it, they are all proud of it, and of the casino money that built it. They enjoy the publicity the Visitor Center has been given by the US government, in tour booklets and on maps, even if the guilt behind the publicity smells oily and leaves a slick residue.

"Come experience the Indian Pueblo. Step back into the past," the government says in their advertising packet.

The Indians understand image. They spend their money on the slit sink and the magic door, but not on electricity or running water up at the pueblo.

The Indians also understand this slippery guilt. This is how they successfully manage to scare everybody into behaving, to keep them from wandering off, to make them pay ten dollars to take a photograph. They affix small ID cards to everybody's cameras like toe tags and threaten to take the cameras away and destroy them in an Indian ceremony with public jeering if unauthorized pictures are taken. This has only happened twice, but both times, the Indians enjoyed themselves and ate hot dogs and beer.

At the Visitor Center, everybody lowers their heads and hands over the ten dollars. The Indians take the money and reserve their energy, hoarding it beneath their cheek bones.

Pink husbands say to their wives, "Ten bucks! This is outrageous. I could just snap a picture with my cell, and they wouldn't even know." The wives shush their husbands, imagining their bodies lying out in the sun, arrow-ridden.

They are on tribal lands, after all. Tribal lands with their own laws, a small, roving group of tribal law officers with as much power as children playing dress-up.

Everybody knows this. They don't say it, and they try not to think it, because the guilt is still there, rushing over them like soapy water, but they know it. When they think the Indians are not watching, they stand up straight, shedding all traces of mansuetude. They imagine the Indians' bodies in a blood-stained, bullet-ridden heap, documented by their digital cameras.

⊕

The bus, bearing the weight of everybody, plus Jennifer and Kathy, crawls up to the pueblo.

Jennifer and Kathy look like sisters. Kathy is a little younger and seems a little happier, though neither of them ever really smiles. Kathy moves quickly, responding to the road with light, quick adjustments, and occasionally flipping her dark hair. Jennifer is thick in the middle, her nipples and stomach meeting roundly, her steps heavy, as if she is wading though something. Kathy and Jennifer do not have names of birds, or seasons, or words separated by hyphens, and this is mildly disappointing to everybody, who resembles golf tees and chubby aliens.

But everybody can also be broken down into further sub-groups:

There is the multi-culti couple, the hip Asian husband and his white-as-paint wife, who both wear shorts and hats and tank-tops. This is a childless couple, as evidenced by their taut bodies and their continuous flirtation, the way the husband's eyes pause at his wife's neckline, embellished with a dirty French word, and the closeness that allows her to keep her hand on the curve of his waist. After this trip to the pueblo, they will go home and look at their digital photographs, and he will tell her how good she looks in her French tank-top, and she will pull it off so he can play with her youthful, smallish breasts.

This couple is the counterpoint to another couple, a German archeologist and an American anthropologist who have not made love in four years, but who have each published several books with glossy photographs and seventeen pages of footnotes in University presses. They are passionate, but not about each other. They talk of their work like they would of a lover or a rapturous meal, and though they struggle not to show it, they both become sexually aroused at the thought of meeting a real Pueblo Indian. They come armed with questions about NAGPRA and Spanish colonization, such that their pre-conceived thoughts poke through their skin like barbs.

The remaining people are a hodgepodge: retired grandparents with thick mid-sections and perms who are vacationing with their grandchildren, teenage boys who walk with their limbs turned inward, every movement signaling their physical shame, and the fussy pink children with hair parted to the side, like news anchors. There is a middle-aged black couple, a tall man and a short wife, both of whom are aware of being the only black people present. They will think fleetingly that they should feel some sort of kinship to the Indians, because they are people of color, but they will not feel anything but the general strangeness of being around a people who live without electricity.

Finally, there is the sensitive man with an unplaceable accent who has read up on the Indians, who keeps calling them "Native Americans," unaware that this particular group of Indians prefers the term "First Americans" and finds his term wholly offensive. He will ask thoughtful questions and take artful pictures, despite the fact that his ancestors once cut off chunks of the Indians' feet as punishment for practicing their religion. But really he cannot be blamed for this, for he was only born, and has since tried to make up for it.

Jennifer, the guide, who is fifty and does not wear a bra, ignores the white woman when she asks again for the air conditioning to be turned on. She understands how to mute their voices in her head. She knows she has to, or else she will snap at them in a way they aren't used to, and she will lose her job. She turns to Kathy.

"Did you see *The Bachelor* last night?"

"Jack and I drove down to get pizza. What'd I miss?"

"It was the finale. Want to know who he picked?"

Kathy nods and turns down the static on her walkie-talkie.

"He picked that blond bimbo. You believe that?"

"Which bimbo? Nancy?"

"No. Kimberly, the dental assistant."

"You're joking," Kathy says, steering the bus up the road to the mesa.

"Nuh-uh," Jennifer says. She tries to imagine herself on such a show, what she would say to the cameras if some white guy put a rose in her hand. Kathy is shacked up with a white truck driver from Comanche, but Jack has lived so long on the pueblo that everyone thinks of him like their own. Jennifer laughs.

"What else happened?" asks Kathy.

"Nothing," Jennifer says. "That was pretty much it."

•

The ride to the top takes less than seven minutes. The bus lurches with the weight of everybody. Turns out golf tees are heavier than they look. Seven minutes. Long enough for several Indians walking up to their houses to pass the bus on foot.

"You comin' over later?" Kathy asks Jennifer.

"Maybe," she says. "I've got at least two more of these." Then Jennifer looks with something dangerously close to disgust, but more obviously boredom, towards everybody. "We're here. Watch your step getting off."

Jennifer waves goodbye to Kathy, who turns back the volume of her walkie-talkie. There is another freight of people waiting for her below, but she must time their pick-up perfectly, or else the two groups will see each other, and the illusion of aloneness and a simpler time will be destroyed.

Everybody gets off with effort, ignoring Kathy. They will not remember her.

The pink children go first, eager to see something, point at it, and announce to everyone what it is. After a few hours on the pueblo, they will whine and turn orange in the sun. They want things: dessert, toys, to push the button on educational placards. They watch a black puppy eating Indian feces and point to it with a skirl.

Jennifer glances at the screaming children out of the corner of her slit-eyes. She does not say anything, but her look conveys the certainty that these children will grow up to be white assholes who make a lot of money. It also communicates to the pink parents that they are solely responsible for their children's welfare up on the pueblo. It says, I will continue with my educational tour even when your children wander too close to the edge. You will watch me chat with Kathy over the radio after your unsupervised toddler gets bit by a rattlesnake.

She puts on her space-age sunglasses, so there is less of her visible to them.

"Welcome to our pueblo," Jennifer says, starting before everybody is completely out of the bus. "Please do not lag behind, because I will walk fast and talk fast, and I will not repeat myself. But I will repeat the rules that you heard down below, that you will only take a photograph when I tell you it is appropriate to take a photograph, and if you do so when it is not the right time, I will take and destroy your camera. Also, do not stray from the group, because you are not allowed to explore the pueblo by yourself. This is because you are on land that is sacred to us, and you are required to treat it with respect. Respect means you stay with me at all times."

Everybody forms a group in front of Jennifer, a triangle with the black people and the sensitive man and the academics at the point, the rest fanning out behind.

They crane their necks to hear her, for she refuses to talk above a normal speaking volume.

Jennifer takes a deep breath, not because she is afraid, but because she has to build up her energy. Her instructions tumble out, one sentence after the other, layered without affect. She has said these things a thousand times, and sometimes she dreams them, or wakes up her husband saying them. "I will take and destroy your camera," she says, rolling over on the thin mattress, and Cliff jabs her in the side with his elbow. He looks at her face, the eyes open but half-lidded, illuminated by moonlight through the open square window. "Wake up," he says. "You're not at work." But in the morning, she will brush out her hair and slide her shorts up her thick legs, and she will step outside the door again to say these things for money.

Cliff is lucky. He works on cars, and parts of cars, and he can go the whole day without ever saying a word to anybody.

Jennifer walks briskly toward the church, the main draw. Everybody tries to keep up with her, but they find it cumbersome to move their bodies in the heat. Their tender, house-conditioned lungs are assaulted by the dust blowing everywhere, unanchored by tree roots or grass.

"This is the Mission of San Felipe," Jennifer says. "That window you can see up in the corner is where the first missionary who came to convert our people was stoned to death. The children of the village called to him, and when he leaned out to give his blessings, they began throwing rocks at him because they did not appreciate his presence here. One large rock struck him in the center of his forehead, and he died, and then the children dragged his body through the street, where everybody celebrated with a parade and singing."

Everybody listens to this story with a shudder, except for the academics who scribble it down in their notebooks, their mouths eagerly filling with saliva. For the black couple, there are disturbing historical echoes, mutilated bodies out on display. They lower their heads solemnly, imagining a brotherhood with this dead priest that they haven't yet felt with the Indians.

The pink husbands' faces tighten. *Animals,* they think, their hearts leaping to patriotic action, pumping out an extra burst of blood, even though the priest was Spanish. What kind of children throw rocks at priests? The wives nervously eye the wild Indian children occasionally running by behind the outhouses. They clutch their arms close to their bodies like dinosaurs.

The multi-culti couple smirks. They are enlightened. They are down with diversity and up for the legalization of marijuana. Good for you, they think. Score one for the Indians.

"Of course," Jennifer says, "Once the Spanish heard about this, they sent a thousand soldiers and subdued our people. They re-established the church as Catholic, punished our people for their religious practice, raped our women, enslaved our men, and forced us to carry trees from that mountain"—Jennifer points to a tiny dot in the distance—"to build their houses and military forts."

"How well has this been documented?" the academics wonder, licking the tips of their pens.

"It's been documented," Jennifer says, evasively. She continues her tour, gesturing to the graveyard in front of the church, with its layers of graves, one built on top of the next, bodies mixed into the foundation of bones, until, Jennifer says, they could no longer build up this wall of the dead.

"Where do you bury people now?" the black woman asks.

"Now we bury most people in a cemetery down below, just at the edge of our land," she says. She does not mention the many Indians who leave this place completely, who get shit jobs out in the world, but better shit jobs, jobs good enough to keep them from coming back. They stay out in the world of electricity and football, running water and reality shows, and when they die they get scattered in white cemeteries with soft green grass and stone angels, in their own hole, where they don't have to share.

Jennifer takes off her sunglasses and opens the tremendous door of the church.

Inside, everybody looks up at the architecture. She explains the circus carnival mix of Catholic saints and wooden crucifixes with the Indian rainbows painted on their walls, their rain clouds swelling against St. Felipe. "Over the years," she tells them, "our people got tired of fighting against the Spanish, and the Spanish got tired of telling us no. They started letting us bring in some of our religion, and we kept on baptizing our children and praying to Jesus Christ. That's how everything gets mixed together at the pueblo."

"What do you do now?" the academics ask. "Whom do you worship? Could you describe a typical service?" They lean forward as if they might fall down upon Jennifer like a lover.

The pink children, bored by these questions, roam the church, staring up at the haunted, elongated faces of saints. They trace the rainbows with their chubby fingers. They clamber to the front of the church, in front of the altar, and plop down at Jennifer's feet. She stares at them for a minute out of the ever thinner line of her eye, and imagines how much closer she will let them come before she kicks them with the rounded toe of her sandal.

"We just do whatever," she answers. "We dance a little. We pray sometimes, like when we really need rain. Which is all the time. Or we just talk to each other, catch up."

This is, of course, a terrible letdown for everybody, everybody who has come from Texas, South Carolina, and Florida to hear about Indians and religious fervor and goat sacrifice, not chitchat and hoedowns at the Church of San Felipe.

As they file out, the multi-culti couple in the rear notes the obnoxious children and smiles, re-affirming their vow never to procreate but to travel and screw as much as humanly possible while respecting and learning about Native peoples everywhere.

●

After the church, Jennifer pauses for a moment while the permed grandparents sample some fry bread from an Indian meth addict, but begins the tour before they are done eating it. "I told you, you have to keep up," she says, stalking off. She won't talk to the meth addict. Fucking meth, she thinks to herself. Makes you crazy. Makes you move like a lizard.

While everybody browses the wares on little tables near the houses, Jennifer talks to a chatty, middle-aged Indian woman named Beth, who works part-time in the towns at a drugstore. Beth is beautiful, with her hair choppily cut and arranged zigzagged atop her head like raven feathers, and with her sexy black halter-top. Everybody looks at, handles, but doesn't buy Beth's pots. A teenage girl, Beth's daughter, stares at everybody from behind a screen door, but doesn't smile and doesn't say anything. The sensitive man ignores a postcard-ready photo-op of the valley surrounding the mesa and instead suddenly takes an artful photograph of Beth's daughter, who immediately disappears.

Jennifer swings around. *"You do not do that,"* she says to the sensitive man. "You do not take pictures of people like that."

"I'm sorry," he says, his face flaming. "I thought you said, I thought we were in a spot where you said we could take photographs."

"It doesn't matter. This isn't a zoo. You ask permission of people before you photograph them."

There is stillness at the top of the pueblo now. The people handling Beth's pots gently return them to the table. Dust whips around the one small tree on the mesa, planted as a joke to see if anything could grow here. In a declivity where just enough rain water collected during the wet season, it has managed to stay alive.

"I'm sorry," the man says. "It won't happen again."

Everybody waits to see if Jennifer will take the camera. They shield themselves with their arms and fanny packs.

But nothing happens. Jennifer takes a breath and moves on. Talking, gesturing. At some point in the tour, an apple and a Twinkie have materialized in her hand. She holds on to them, even uses them to point at specific structures. "We build up, not out," she says, the Twinkie sweating against its plastic wrapper. "This is why you see all our houses are two and three stories, with small rooms."

Everybody knows that Jennifer is holding her lunch. Her distinctly un-Indian lunch. Everybody wonders if she is sending them a message. I'm done with you people, the message says. Just two more houses, and I dump you suckers with Kathy, and I'm on my lunch break. How rude, they think.

Jennifer doesn't think of her lunch. She thinks of her mouth saying the meaningless words, and how each word stamps a second, bringing her closer to the end of another hour.

"Where do *you* live?" a pink woman asks. "Close to here?" At the same moment, she looks away at her teenage son, leaning over the edge of the mesa. "Mason, get away from there." The boy ignores her, steps closer to the edge. "GIT. A-WAY. FROM. THEYERE." The mother has forgotten all about Jennifer and her house.

Jennifer motions to Randall Hanson's house. "There," she says. "That one's mine." Everybody turns to admire it.

She pictures her real house, with its cool, dark walls, and imagines lying down for a quick nap after lunch, before the next tour. She tries to guess if Cliff made the bed before he left for work.

•

Near the end of the tour, they stop and look at a *kiva* where the men hold their tribal meetings. A thick white ladder leans against it, pointing skyward.

"Men only," Jennifer says, indicating the ladder the Indian men use to enter the building, and the small hole in the wall they use to communicate with the women outside. She thinks about the hole sometimes, and how much she hates talking to Cliff through it, the way it makes his voice sound nasal and distant. It seems dangerous to her somehow. As if their voices were being strained through the narrow passage. Diluted. Yet she also thinks how much easier it would be if she could communicate with these people through it. She could pretend she was talking to anybody. Brad Pitt. The guy from *The Bachelor.*

After explaining about the men in the *kiva,* Jennifer tells a mildly sexist joke she has been instructed to tell, but, without modulation and verbal cues, nobody laughs.

From below, Kathy's bus starts up with a choke. In a few minutes, she will arrive with the next group of people and take this group back to their cars. She will have a Diet Dr. Pepper in her hand, and she will explain to this group their options.

They can: A) Tip Jennifer, watch her blow on her hands to ward off the evil money spirits, and ride back in the bus. B) Tip Jennifer, and then walk down the graveled road back to the Visitor Center, where they can purchase mementos of their visit and leave a tip for Kathy as well, who doesn't feel the need to ward off spirits, but who is hoping to buy an iPad. Or C) Tip Jennifer, and climb down an ancient stone stairway once used by the Indians to haul up water, though nobody uses it anymore now that they have trucks and a road. Beth's other little daughter,

Brittany, who is ten, will guide them, hold the women's purses, tell them where to wedge their feet and hands. Brittany will bound down like an antelope, and watch while they cling to the sides of the cliffs in terror. Brittany, with bangs like sea kelp, will get help if they fall and break their spines. No one ever goes down this way.

Jennifer stands next to the *kiva* and wonders if any of these people will try the staircase. She hasn't used it since she was a teenager, following Cliff on a dare. Maybe the professors will climb down, she thinks. For authenticity.

"We are almost done," Jennifer says. "Just one more house."

Next to the *kiva*, an old Indian couple is renovating their house, adding a mixture of mud and hay to the outer wall with the palms of their hands. They move like wind-up dolls, steadily reaching down into a wheelbarrow for the mud and smearing it clockwise into the wall. The husband barely glances up to acknowledge everybody. His wife pointedly says, "Afternoon, Jennifer," as if Jennifer is alone.

As Jennifer explains what they are doing, how everything is made by hand, the mud ovens, the pots, the heaven-pointing ladders, all with elements from the pueblo, one pink lady angles herself closer to the Indian couple.

She pulls out her camera. With a proud smile on her face, as if to announce her respect, her ability to remember the rules and instructions, the lady looks at the couple and interrupts Jennifer's narration.

"Excuse me. Can I take your picture?"

The old man looks a little embarrassed, and wipes the mud from his hands. His wife ignores the woman and keeps working.

"Sure. I guess," he says. He widens his stance a bit, as if he is posing as a football player.

"Oh, you don't have to stop what you're doing. Just keep building your house," the woman says. She adjusts her camera lens and crouches.

Nearby, the sensitive man watches, waiting for a reprimand from Jennifer that never comes.

As the woman clicks away, the man and his wife resume their methodical work, aware of being watched. They are used to the presence of observers on the pueblo; they have seen them many times, buying key chains, leaving crumbs of fry bread that ravens later eat in the branches of the tree. They ignore them as they add to their houses, maintaining them, the wives giving their husbands blue rags to hang in the highest windows, new rooms to sit awkwardly out to the side, to house more children. "Paint the doors blue or red," the women tell them, and the men do it.

The camera snaps and whirs.

"Could you try to smile?" the pink woman asks.

Acknowledgments

Many thanks to the editors of the publications listed below for first publishing these stories:

"Hibernators" in *Minnesota Review*

"New Year" in *Witness*

"Victory Forge" in *The Sun*

"Sour Milk" in *52 Stories*

"Continuity in Filmmaking," as "Remind Me To Show You Your Face" in *Swill*

"Adwok, Pantokrator" in *Michigan Quarterly Review*

"MacArthur Park" in *Red Wheelbarrow*

"The Yana Land" in *The Literary Review*

"Everything Gets Mixed Together at the Pueblo," originally published in *Crab Orchard Review* and later anthologized in *Tremors: New Fiction by Iranian American Writers*

I am deeply grateful to everyone at The Ohio State University Press for their tremendous kindness and support, especially Erin McGraw, Malcolm Litchfield, Eugene O'Connor, Tara Cyphers, Laurie Avery, Linda Patterson Blackwell, and Kathy Edwards.

My thanks to the editors who first helped shape these stories, including Heather Steffen, David Armstrong, Luc Saunders, Cal Morgan, Rob Pierce, Sean Craven, Jonathan Freedman, Victoria Johnson, Ken Weisner, Minna Proctor, and Jon Tribble.

To Lyle Dechant, Amanda Alley, Anne Harris, Meagan Brothers—the best first readers anyone could hope for. Because they edit with green ink, and because there's usually pie afterwards.

For a multitude of personal and professional kindnesses: Mollie Glick. Jessamyn Smyth. Julie Schwietert Collazo. Harrison Solow. David Haynes. Greg Olear. Cynthia Hawkins. Persis Karim. Anita Amirrezvani. Ken Holt. Karol Nielsen. Beth Hoffman. Paula Yoo. Becky Sain. Madhusudan Katti. Chris Clarke. Arvind and Minal. Heather, Hannah, and Flip.

Thanks to my friends and colleagues at Manhattanville College, Jeff Bens and Mark Nowak, especially, and to my students for the inspiration, the patience, and the faith in all of us, always, trying to be better storytellers.

To Mom, Dad, Joe, and Andrea. I love you guys.

To Denali, who knows.

And most of all, to Lyle. For coming up that mountain.